Death Reports to a Health Resort

to a Health Resort

The Ninth Anty Boisjoly Mystery

Death Reports to a Health Resort

The Ninth Anty Boisjoly Mystery

CHAPTER ONE

A Scorning Warning of a Mourning Morning

"Anty, you must go to Epping immediately. Your uncle has been accused of murder — again."

To be fair to the uncle under appraisal, he had never actually been accused of murder before. To be fair to my mother, who was delivering this edict by telephone, he had been accused of destruction of property, verbal assault on a constable, non-verbal assault on another constable, sedition, causing a disturbance, and, in the interests of accuracy, several poorly-mounted instances of *attempted* murder, and these are occasions we know about.

"Epping, you say?" I checked. "If you think that will help, but have I an uncle in Epping?"

"No."

"Right oh."

"I am referring to Postlewick Pimsloe, my cousin by your great aunt Mimi," Mama clarified the above-mentioned chap in question.

"Uncle Pim lives in Holland Park," I pointed out, helpfully.

"I know that he lives in Holland Park, Anty." Mama's impatient sigh came over the line like a castle class locomotive giving its steam breaks a chance to put its feet up. "He is at his health retreat, where there has been a death under most unusual circumstances, and some insufferable detective inspector has decided to dispense with the formalities and arrest your Uncle Pim."

"Unusual circumstances, you say." I knew then why it was that Mama had called me directly at the Kensington pied-à-terre, when under normal circumstances if she wishes to communicate something she just waits until we're in close enough proximity to express her views in the form of long, judgemental silences. Death by quirky circs has become something of a family area of expertise for me, of late, in much the same way that Mama specialises in crushing the dreams of the naive at the baccarat table in Monte Carlo.

"I don't know the details, Anty. I just need you to go to Eden Bliss Paradise Health Resort in Epping Forest and represent the family interests."

"I've heard tell of the place, now I know of whom we speak," I said. "Uncle Pim has written me on and off over the years when he finds himself at what he describes as 'Dante's ninth circle of wellness'. Last year around this time he asked me to engage a team of oriental mercenaries and effect a rescue."

"Your uncle is of a very anxious disposition," euphemised Mama.

"He's potty as a one-stop pot shop."

"I defer to your domain expertise," backhanded Mama. "In any case, these little retreats from temptation normally do him tremendous good."

"I know they do," I agreed. "It's been months since he last appeared in court on charges of shouting obscenities at a horse."

"I trust you to treat the matter with discretion, Anty," said Mama, adding, with reference to some fancy or other, "We already have enough scandal in this family."

"Count on me for complete confidentiality, favourite living parent," I said to my poor, widowed mother. "I shall have Vickers burn the telephone as soon as we ring off."

My valet was standing by, as it happened, the moment my mother wished me a warm "Now, don't dally," doubtless fighting back the tears, and the line crackled and closed.

"You heard, Vickers?"

"Yes, sir." The Boisjoly gentlemen's gentleman's personal gentleman has served in the role since before my father's father first needed a loyal retainer standing by with a whisky and soda when he'd done speaking to his mother. "Shall I pack for the week, sir?"

"Difficult to say." I sipped meditatively. "You know how these things go — you remember those dual locked room murders in Canterfell last year."

"No, sir."

It would come to him. Vickers stopped curating current events around the coronation of King George and his memory was now a happy happenstance of random chance.

"Well, you must remember the impenetrable mysteries in Hoy, in the Peak District — we were there for nearly a week only a few months ago."

"Was that the occasion on which we were compelled to lock a reporter from *The Times* society page in the coal cellar?"

"No, that was Cuff Lincoln's bachelor do," I reminded him, "which was last night. No, in Hoy we untangled two impossible deaths thought, by the locals, to have been caused by a curse, and by our friend and favourite flatfoot, Inspector Wittersham, to be the work of Carnaby, London's finest club steward."

"Of course."

"In short, Vickers, I can't say how long we'll be in Epping, so you'd best pack for at least a week and release the journalist from the coal cellar — better to err on the side of caution, in these matters."

"Indeed, sir."

❦

"Do you think we should assume a dour countenance?" I asked Vickers from my side of a first-class compartment bound for the market town of Epping. "Or rend our vestments or some such?"

"I would remind you, sir, that you're wearing your last serviceable travel tweeds until our tailor returns from his rest cure at Bethlem." Vickers, also dressed in a natty tall twill, sat in the direction of travel, as he must do if we don't want him dozing off and waking with the sensation of falling from London to Exeter.

"I merely wonder if we shouldn't make an effort to assimilate," I said. "Eden Bliss Paradise Health Resort isn't one of your weekend retreats, where the genteel go to take the waters and bathe in mud as society penance for a large end to the social season. It's for hard cases, like Uncle Pim and that bloke, you know — wandering eye, always looks like he's about to tell Mistress."

"His Royal Highness the Prince of Wales, sir."

"That's the chap," I twigged. "Hard cases like that. They take one look at the boisterous Boisjoly blush and, likely as anything else, the doorman will rough me up and chuck me into an alley."

I was short of my thirtieth year and, depending on the time of day, could pass for a chap ten years younger still. Depending on the time of morning, mind you, I could easily be mistaken for a career sailor in his late sixties. In the moment, I was certainly not presenting as the sort of mouldering vessel of diminished chances that is the raw resource of Eden Bliss Paradise Health Resort, what with my slim stature and jolly nature, chestnut hair and hazel eyes and Boisjoly eyebrows that look like they enjoy a nice surprise.

Vickers, who has aged like a fine Viking settlement, also appears remarkably robust and — again, for his age — straight and of strict habits, like a silver-haired steeple.

"I should think, sir, under the circumstances, that an exception will be made," suggested Vickers.

"That's probably so," I agreed. "Uncle Pim's a valued customer. He's been going to Eden Bliss Paradise for six years — since the day he had an unbroken series of late finishers at Goodwood in 1923 and tried to uncork a track tout."

"Mister Pimsloe has a quick temper," surmised Vickers.

"Quick is the word, Vickers," I confirmed. "Like lightning that's sat on something sharp. It's never without some sort of trigger, though, such as a slow horse or bad bounce of the ball at roulette or a short straw."

"He likes to gamble."

"Bit of an understatement," I said. "Unless you'd also say that the sun enjoys rising occasionally in the east. If all's going well, mind you, he's merely another eccentric English gentleman who fancies scones and finding racing tips in the stars, the distribution of fallen leaves, the order in which foreign delegations are presented to the king, and in which buses arrive on Oxford Street."

The cinema of scenery soon shifted from dusty, bustly London to low and listless suburbs and then to leafy, lush woodland sharing the screen intermittently with fertile fields of mixed farming. Then the rails were the border between the people's forest to our left and, to our right, the little stone and daub Chigwells and Woodfords and Loughtons of Essex, each nestled neatly around a pointy church and a stubby pub on a cobbled market square.

"I trust you haven't spared the munitions, Vickers," I remembered to mention. "Eden Bliss Paradise Health Resort trades — openly and shamelessly — on a reputation as a refuge from temptation. There's no whisky allowed, not to mention tobacco, rich foods, light entertainments, sports betting, or bawdy limericks. Uncle Pim describes it as an inquisition prison, with comparatively progressive views on immolation."

"There is a store of Glen Glennegie in the boot box and a selection of burgundies distributed among your suits," inventoried Vickers. "I have eight bottles of serviceable champagne in my own luggage, there are full flasks in your morning, afternoon, evening, and occasional coats and you have one on your person, in your inside left breast pocket. There is also a bottle of Courvoisier 1910 and a wineskin, but I have forgotten where."

"That should see us through the night," I judged. "I feel quite sure that Uncle Pim is exaggerating conditions at the front — the place costs more than the Paris Ritz, including damage deposit. It's in a choice country clearing in an old-growth forest and it caters to spending society's most exclusive soak, choate, gambler, and stoke."

"It sounds most luxurious."

"I expect it is," I agreed. "If Uncle Pim genuinely disliked it all that much, he could always just leave."

❦

The exclusivity of Eden Bliss Paradise Health Resort was jealously guarded by miles of packed English jungle, overgrown and underbrushed, wet and slippery and dark beneath an unbroken canopy of dripping green.

From Epping we hired a hansom who was prepared to take us only as far as the homestead of Mister Livesy, the single outsider entrusted with the actual location of Eden Bliss Paradise and the means to get there — a two-wheeled sulky wagon drawn mercilessly over rock, river, and felled tree alike by the world's largest Clydesdale by half. Where the forest floor wasn't coarse and broken it was spongy and slow. A cold damp shimmered on every surface, animal, vegetable, and Boisjoly.

After several hours of this we arrived at the rim of a steamy, timeless valley, from which rose an ominous mist and the squawks and squeals of prehistoric wildlife. All else was a sort of statutory silence, imposed by the sound-absorbing qualities of brush and briar.

"Where's the hotel?" I asked Mister Livesy.

Our guide turned his wizened, oak-bark countenance on me, withdrew a pipe that appeared to have been carved from a hoof, and said, "Heh."

The sulky could go no further and so we began unloading our trunks and valises when an uncanny, otherworldly rustling approached rapidly through the long grass separating us from the basin of the valley. It moved with terrifying rapidity and was invisible but for the disturbance in the green pool of vegetation as it described a path directly for us.

A moment later, the creature burst from the curtain of grass — it was a saggy, squat basset hound, huffing and woofing and slapping itself with its always-surprising-no-matter-how-many-times-you-see-a-basset-hound long ears.

The dog stopped at my boot box, first, and then served Vickers with a cold, accusing glare. Then he examined the steamer trunks, at each of which he shook his head in despair for the young men of today, and then he brought the famous sense of smell to bear on our persons, expressing his verdict with a profoundly disappointed, hang-dog look, even for a basset hound.

"You gentlemen carrying any contraband?" asked Mister Livesy.

"Are we carrying any contraband, Vickers?" I deferred the point, as I was busy scratching the dog behind the ears. "By which, of course I mean, anything that would be regarded by His Majesty's revenue service as susceptible to import duty."

"Alcohol, tobacco, any victuals of any kind," specified Mister Livesy. "Diogenes here won't let you past with any of it."

"Ah, but you see, Diogenes," I addressed the basset hound, "we're not patients. We've come to assist the police in their enquiries."

"You here about the murder?"

"Exactly." I continued to press my case with Diogenes. "There, you see? Mister Livesy vouches for us."

"You're no policeman."

"Thank you."

"There's a detective-inspector already here. I brought him in this morning," added Livesy.

"Yes, I know there is, Mister Livesy — I'm operating under a different mandate, to sort of keep the inquiry on an even keel…" I beckoned him move closer to myself and the dog. "I wouldn't want this to get about, but I've been asked to look into this by no less authority than my mother."

"Your mother."

"I prefer to invoke her name only if it's strictly necessary."

"Mister Boisjoly?"

We all looked to the valley to see a robust and rounded, tightly packed blonde stiletta in laboratory whites and lipsticky reds sashaying towards us through the grass.

"This one," I gestured to the self under advisement. "Are you the detective-inspector?"

"I'm Nurse Dalimore," said, if she was to be believed, Nurse Dalimore. "Destiny Dalimore."

"Right oh." I resumed adult height and extended a distinctly doggy hand, which she nevertheless took. "Anthony Boisjoly. Boisjoly is counter-intuitively pronounced 'Beaujolais', like the wine region, but everyone calls me Anty, with the exception of a barmaid at the Criterion who refers to me as 'Twofist', in accordance with a system of her own design."

"Your uncle has told me so much about you — I can't believe even half of it's true," swooned Nurse Dalimore. "I'm sure he's just being unkind."

"The possibility can't be entirely discounted," I acknowledged with a sage nod. "I say, how did you know my name?"

"Inspector Wittersham said to expect you."

"Inspector Ivor Wittersham, of the Wittersham Wittershams?" I marvelled. "Always dressed for a rainy funeral? Moustache that appears to have been drawn on while pursuing subject through unlit warehouse?"

"I believe so," ventured the nurse dubiously. "When he learned that Mister Pimsloe was your uncle he said that you'd be along shortly. It was Mister Livesy that sent your uncle's telegram to you."

I have a sense for the silent language of the subtle gesture, and I was detecting something eerily, even aggressively intimate in Nurse Dalimore's manner. It was manifest in the depth of her stare and the slight angle of her head and the fact that she had yet to let go of my hand.

"In fact the telegram was sent to central dispatch," I gently extracted my paw from the trap, "but I was the first disappointment on rotation. Who died?"

"The inspector asked me not to answer your questions until you two have spoken," Nurse Dalimore intoned with one part hurt to two parts pique. "Is he always so testy?"

"Not at all," I assured her. "Sometimes he must sleep."

"Excuse me, sir." Vickers made a nervous debut. "Pardon me, Miss. Sir, Mister Livesy is offering to take charge of provisions."

"Ah, yes, Nurse Dalimore, my man, Vickers," I presented. "Vickers has packed a few medicinal unctions and salves which your border patrol has identified, doubtless defining his duties in the broadest possible scope, as contraband."

"There's no alcohol allowed at Eden Bliss Paradise, Mister Boisjoly," said the nurse with earnest resolve. "No tobacco, alcohol — no material vices or temptations of any kind. Even the slightest exception could set the programme back months."

"Of course," I acknowledged the virtue of necessity. "Very well, Vickers, make whatever arrangements you deem fit with Mister Livesy."

"I regret, sir, that I was unclear — Mister Livesy is proposing to discard the champagne and wine — in a ditch."

"A ditch? *Chateau Sorine 1912?* In a ditch?" I then whispered confidentially to Nurse Dalimore, "Inform the inspector that I have identified the killer."

"And he intends to use the Glen Glennegie as fuel for his generator." Vickers' voice cracked with emotion.

"What do you suggest?"

"I would propose, sir, that I accompany Mister Livesy and see the goods returned safely to Kensington, before rejoining you here."

"But, what if I need to dress for dinner? Or shave?"

"I shall endeavour to return as expeditiously as possible," said Vickers. "I can't say how long it will take to make arrangements."

"Just so long as none of it winds up in a ditch," I said. "Donate the lot to an orphanage, if you must."

❦

"What ho, Inspector."

Inspector Ivor Wittersham, of Scotland Yard (and the Wittersham Wittershams), was pacing and retracing a muddy path, his pipe clenched in his teeth.

I had descended with Dalimore and Diogenes into the misty little depression which, I would later learn, was the communal compound of the resort. Around it was a collection of shacks and sheds and haphazard housing, and in the middle was the corpse of a gnarled old oak which, though it had died of old age many years ago, still supported a tree house some twenty feet in the air. The still, hazy, hovering damp and disquiet afforded the scene a grim, Grimm quality, where a cottage made of candy and a smooth-talking wolf wouldn't raise an eyebrow.

Dalimore left to do something nursy in one of the ground-level buildings and Diogenes stayed by me.

"Boisjoly." Ivor looked about to, presumably, ensure that nobody heard the following, "I'm glad you're here."

"In all candour, Inspector, I'm not," I confessed. "They took away my vitals and valet. How is it that you have tobacco?"

"I don't." Ivor puffed a gruff of clean, angry air through his unlit pipe. "That animal found all I had."

"He has an excellent nose — went straight for the Glen Glennegie. Who died?"

"Doctor Marvin Smick." Ivor withdrew his pipe and crossed his arms and surveyed the muddy grounds as though still trying to come to terms with something. "He was the owner and mastermind of this... resort. It takes in your lot's tragically under-disciplined and overindulgent and, apparently, wrings out the poison and sends them home in time for the next social season. I expect you must have summered here as a child."

"Never been," I corrected. "But, as you've already determined, I have an uncle among the inmates. Is that why you're glad I'm here? Do you require an interpreter for Ticked Toff?"

"Doctor Smick was killed there." Ivor pointed with his pipe at one of the higher shack towers. "All alone, in a locked room, twenty feet above the ground."

"You don't mean to say, Inspector..."

"Yes, Mister Boisjoly," he did, indeed, mean to say, "this is the most vexing case of locked room murder I've ever seen."

CHAPTER TWO

A Very Chary Adversary in the Airy Sanctuary

"He apparently called it his sanctuary."

The inspector and I had climbed a rope ladder, Ivor employing his military background and me leveraging my experience in swinging from chandeliers to gain access to a wooden box that presented as a treehouse built by a child with little imagination and few resources. The floor space was roughly that of a London taxi and it had a door on one side and a window on the other — in fact, it had a doorway on one side and a window frame on the other; there was neither door nor glass. Well-ventilated, though, with easy access to local amenities and plenty of privacy.

"This is where I found him." Ivor looked at a spot on the floor.

"Where you found him? You were here when Doctor Smick became an exemplary existentialist?"

"No, I was called in after it happened, but I had to climb up here to recover the remains," said Ivor. "That rope ladder had been pulled up after him, and none of the others are in any condition to climb trees."

"I see no blood."

"No — he was killed by some sort of fast-acting poison."

"Ah, well then, Inspector, I believe I've repaid my substantial fee already," I announced. "He wasn't killed here. He consumed the poison on the ground, and then climbed up to his sanctuary before it had time to get its sleeves properly rolled up."

Ivor shook his head firmly. "He'd been up here for an entire day. No food, no drink."

"Just whisky?" I marvelled at the man's restraint.

"Nothing at all," wearied Ivor. "He apparently believed in leading by example — he was abstaining from all temptation."

"Slow-acting poison, then," I concluded. "You're welcome."

"Several witnesses — just about everyone in the place — heard him call out at the last minute," stymied Ivor. "With a slower poison he'd have time to climb down and, possibly, get medical attention."

"Well, then, Inspector, I wish it wasn't me who has to shatter your illusions of the dearly departed, but he wasn't leading by any sort of example," I concluded. "Whatever killed him, he brought up here with him. Probably boiled sweets, or some similar choking hazard. Did you find any lolly sticks?"

"Apparently, he couldn't have had anything with him when he came up here," persisted Ivor, "the dog sees to that. No one's allowed to bring anything into the sanctuary, the dog checked him when he climbed up and he would have been seen if he'd come back down."

"Surely not." From the window I could see only a misty meadow floor to the little valley and a few scattered shacks and shanties. "Why would the patients linger in this desolate place? They'd have gone to the tea room or the games rooms or library."

"There is no tea room. No library."

"The dining room, then," I suggested. "Or their own private suites in the main hall."

"This desolate place is the entire resort," said Ivor. "No golf club, no tennis courts, no en suite apartments."

"Have you looked?" I asked. "I was given to understand that Eden Bliss Paradise Health Resort was the most exclusive renovation station in the south-east, not counting that secret facility inside Westminster Bridge to which Scotland Yard sends all its inspectors."

"I've told you, repeatedly, that there is no such place."

"And yet," I said, "rumours persist."

"I've only ever heard that from you."

"Because I'm persistent."

"This compound is the entirety of Eden Bliss Paradise Health Resort." Ivor, evading the issue, made expansive reference to the grounds beneath us. "I'm led to understand that privation is central to Doctor Smick's patented cure."

"This is what my Uncle Pim led me to understand," I said. "I assumed he was exaggerating."

"Is he given to exaggeration?" Reflexively, Ivor drew heavily on his pipe, creating an amusing whistling sound.

"Only in certain areas," I specified. "He's never, in my presence, overstated an outstanding debt, but I have heard him characterise a racing tip from the paddock as a solemn vow from a loving God, and the subsequent failure of that tip to pay off as clear and concrete evidence of a far-reaching conspiracy. He also told my mother that you've accused him of murder."

Ivor knocked nothing out of his pipe against the door frame before swinging out onto the rope ladder. "That wasn't an exaggeration."

❧

"Doctor Smick was a visionary."

The nursely duties that Destiny Dalimore had to perform weren't as cartesian as I'd imagined — there was appreciably less apportioning of pills and weighing of samples than there was setting fire to fragrant bamboo shoots and breathing in the smoke and saying "Oooommmwaah" or something meaning very much the same thing.

We were in the Fulfilment Lodge, which was high-ceilinged, well-appointed, and airy, for a weatherboard chicken coop, furnished with pasha pillows and dust. I had the only milking stool while the nurse moved about setting fire to things and arranging brass pots and ceramic bowls, and adding to the atmosphere with a clay mortar of dried birch leaves which she pestled to a powder before dangling a glass pendant over it.

"Now he is at one with the vision," she said, seemingly in passing.

"Just a bit prematurely," I prompted. "Most of us prefer uniting with the vision a bit later in life, once it's had a chance to play the smaller venues."

"Yes." Dalimore stirred the leaves with a stick that she found on the ground, or had placed there earlier for this purpose. "Doctor Smick was deliberately denied the full breadth of his journey of discovery." She appeared to puzzle over this momentarily before translating, "You'd say that he was murdered."

"No, I wouldn't," I differed only slightly. "I'd probably say something like 'someone discounted his retirement', or 'a person or persons unknown have set a firm date set for his eulogies.' It's how I cope. I understand that you were present for the announcement?"

"He was in his sanctuary." Nurse Dalimore gazed in the rough direction of up. "He called out to me — 'Nurse Dalimore!' — he never called me Destiny in front of the guests — 'I've been injected with poison. Fetch a doctor.'"

"Wasn't he a doctor?" I enquired.

"I think he meant a traditionally trained doctor," speculated the nurse. "And one who hadn't been poisoned."

"I see. And where did the poison come from?"

"He didn't mention." Dalimore finished abusing the dried leaves, which she now gathered into a little ceremonial thurible. "He sounded pressed for time."

"Inspector Wittersham is convinced that he could have brought nothing with him up to his treehouse. Is that your view, too?"

"Sanctuary," corrected Dalimore. "Nothing is allowed in the sanctuary, and Diogenes sees to it that the rule is strictly observed."

"Diogenes is, presumably, Doctor Smick's dog," I said. "Doubtless he made an exception."

"He was provided by Mister Livesy," contradicted the nurse. "And Diogenes would never show any favouritism — he is a dog of a very egalitarian spirit."

"A pomeranian acquaintance of mine — you probably don't know her, she lives in Bayswater under the name Nibbleit — one day gave me a clear and uncompromising insight into the duplicitous and, dare I say it, triplicitous capabilities to which the canine mind can extend itself."

"Diogenes has never failed in his duties." Nurse Dalimore lowered the thurible into an ornate brass vessel of liquid simmering over a tallow flame.

"Neither had Nibbleit," I assured her. "At least, not according to her interpretation thereof, which restricted them to preventing the postman from ever reaching the front door. I witnessed her in action on several occasions, for Nibbleit is the sole housemate of the maiden aunt of Cores Pommeroy, chap from my club."

"Tea, Mister Boisjoly?" asked Dalimore.

"Do you have tea?"

"Not as you're probably familiar with it." She set out two stone cups and raised the brass urn from the fire, amplifying its unique perfume of forest and foliage and, if it had an odour, vertigo. "You were telling me about Pores Pommeroy?"

"Cores. I was. He made a point of visiting the maiden aunt any Saturday we were going to the courses and collecting her racing tips."

"Had she a talent for the track?" asked Dalimore as she poured out cups of what looked like pond water, only speckier.

"None at all," I said. "Her inside information, while extensive, was invariably incorrect and in any case ended with the 1906 Epsom Derby — she kept advising us to put our shirts on Dingwall who, incidentally, didn't show in 1906, either, and in fact he came in tenth. But Cores' view is that there's no present like the time, so we'd promenade the ancestor and her pom through the gardens of Pembridge Square and take enthusiastic note of her counsel."

"Thank you Mister Boisjoly," Dalimore took up her cup of leaf water, "I feel uplifted."

"Almost there, Nurse," I assured her. "Last Goodwood and last turn round the park, who should we spot but the postman, making a break for the front door of Aunty Pommeroy's stucco frontage. We were behind the high iron gates of the park, though, and the Pommeroy Pom could do little more than yap in a piercing pitch."

"Diogenes rarely barks," noted Dalimore.

"That's because he has gravitas," I said. "Nibbleit has only a carrying soprano. Until, that is, the postman was set upon by a Scottish Terrier and a cur of questionable parentage, both of whom were known to the police, and one of whom had lost his sense of smell and the kind disposition with which all dogs are born to a case of juvenile canine distemper, and the other of whom was doubtless a product of poor parenting and the class system."

"What happened?"

"Nibbleit happened," I said. "The moment she saw her postman facing a real threat, she went into a whirling rage. She hurled herself at the fence and, somehow, ended up on the other side of it. In the next moment or less she was between the postman and these trespassers, flashing fangs, haltered hide, spitting and hissing a deadly resolve. She looked just like a feather duster storming the Bastille."

"Was she badly hurt?" worried Dalimore, wide-eyed over her steaming swamp water.

"Not even slightly," I reported. "The larger dogs, doubtless knowing where they could source a lower-risk postman, sued for peace, and were last seen seeking the higher ground of Notting Hill."

"Nibbleit saved the postman?" deduced Dalimore.

"She did," I took up my tea as a matter of form. "So you see, dogs can appear to hold very different views of the bipeds in their society, once budgeting for considerations such as territory, external threats, and steak."

"I see."

"There you go," I raised my teacup conclusively. "Privately, Diogenes may have taken a very lenient attitude towards Doctor Smick."

"Yes, I see what you mean." Dalimore nodded distractedly and drew on her tea. This gave her pause as she appeared to realise what she'd done, and she looked at her cup for a moment as though seeing it for the first time. "But I feel quite sure that Diogenes gave Doctor Smick no quarter. In fact, I'd say that they harboured a marked dislike for one another, and just before he went up to the sanctuary Diogenes made him turn out his pockets."

"Was he carrying anything? A bottle of whisky, for example, or a vial with a skull and crossbones on the label?"

"No, and there was nothing in his pockets, but it turned out that a hawthorn berry had found its way into his trouser cuffs."

"Insidious things."

Dalimore nodded at her tea. "Diogenes is very committed to a consistent application of the rules."

"In fact, now you put it in those terms," I said, "so was Nibbleit. I recall that the very next thing she did after rescuing the postman was bite him on the calf."

"You're not drinking your tea, Mister Boisjoly."

"You first."

Nurse Dalimore closed her eyes and, to my amazement, drank deeply of her cup of artisanal puddle.

"I feel closer to nature already," she said in what I regard as an ambiguous endorsement.

"So, you definitely saw Doctor Smick climb up to his sanctuary, did you?"

"We all did."

"Yes, Inspector Wittersham tells me that the doctor practised what he prattled."

"He would often go to his sanctuary to meditate," confirmed the nurse, "but there were also occasions, such as today, when he would retreat up there."

"Retreat?"

"And pull the ladder up after him."

"From what was he escaping?" I asked. "Tea?"

"Guests of Eden Bliss Paradise Health Resort are often reluctant to free themselves of the vexations and temptations which have been their companions for so very long."

"You refer to drinking and smoking and eating all the butter."

"As very good examples, yes." Dalimore raised the tea phial in a threatening manner.

"I'm fine for the moment." I waved away the offer. "I'm letting the sediment gather — it's my favourite bit."

At that instant a worrying cloud passed over the face of Nurse Dalimore and I briefly feared that she was going to have a moment of mourning, a social setting for which I have few talents. Then, however, the dial turned to something more like inspired confusion.

"Why, Mister Boisjoly…" she gazed with matronly concern at something some three inches behind my forehead, "…you have a smudge on your aura."

"I know." I nodded in brave resignation. "It's been like that since I got back from Monte Carlo. My man, Vickers, has tried everything short of sandpaper."

"I can help you."

"Oh, no, I wouldn't want to impose," I said. "We're just going to get my tailor to work around it."

"I sense that you're not without demons of your own, Mister Boisjoly."

"You know my mother?" I marvelled. "I'll tell her you said hello."

"You must give yourself over to the liberty of abstinence." Dalimore's eyes widened as though they, and they alone, understood the immensity of what she was proposing.

"Right oh, Nurse," I agreed. "Conditional that you spend next boat race night with the Oxford supporters and a tanker ship of champagne. It'll give you valuable insights into my condition."

"Why, Mister Boisjoly…" The nurse cast her eyes coyly into her cup of runoff. "I couldn't possibly. Not so soon after what's happened."

"Oh, right. I see," I lied, for I was mystified by her response in a way that I felt would reward future demystification. "You were close, were you?"

"Strictly professionally," fumbled Dalimore. "I admired him to the ends of the earth."

"That is a substantial amount of admiration," I acknowledged. "Particularly for just the one person. I take it you carried the full burden of admiration."

"Hmmm?"

"You implied that the doctor took to his sanctuary to retreat from a confrontation with the guests," I reminded her.

"That's true." Dalimore nodded absently. "We'd just completed one of our group sessions, which are typically quite passionate, but this one took a particularly spirited turn during the Unladening."

"Unladening?"

"One by one, the guests take the floor to release themselves of the ire they hold for those they feel have wronged them."

"Oh yes? We have something very like that at the Juniper," I said. "Although it's less an 'unladening' and more a 'kicking off about Budge Willoughby never making good on a loan.' If anything the event soon becomes quite a generous ladening."

"Indeed, that's often how these sessions end as well," said Dalimore. "Although today was especially impassioned, I think."

"Was anyone among the guests especially ladened?"

"Your uncle," recalled Dalimore, with worryingly little hesitation. "He threatened to kill Doctor Smick."

CHAPTER THREE

Leave Horses to Courses or Soon Know What Remorse Is

"To be completely fair to Uncle Pim, he's threatened to murder just about everyone, at least once," I said to the inspector when we met once again beneath the arbour harbour. "He once told me he'd feed me to the ogre in the coal cellar if I didn't stop making tents out of his great coats in the library."

"Cold-blooded thing to say to a child."

"This was last year," I said. "Furthermore, I've since had Vickers check — Uncle Pim doesn't even have a coal cellar, just a bunker off the kitchen, and it's nowhere near big enough for an ogre."

"What's his particular vice, by the way?" asked Ivor, puffing pointlessly on his pipe. "The horses, did you say?"

"He does like a flutter on a mudder, but in my view his real flaw is that he's a poor loser, in the same manner and to similar degree that Othello was a poor listener."

"Has he ever become violent?"

"Once punched a horse."

"A horse?"

"Square on the fleshy hindquarters. Uncle Pim is very spontaneous in his reactions," I explained. "He happened to be walking through the parade ring at Ally Pally when, coming the other way, was Tealy Deal, a moodily unreliable but occasionally cunning three-year-old on whose performance in the fifth Uncle Pim had just made a very generous donation to a tout named Oy Roy. Had it been the next day or even later in the afternoon they might have passed one another with a cordial, sporting nod, but as it was the wound was fresh and feelings were hot and Tealy Deal, in that moment, issued what to Uncle Pim sounded an indifferent, even mocking snort, as horses will."

"And so he punched the horse?"

"Who was doubtless a student of the Sermon on the Mount," I continued, "for he simply snorted once again, turned the other cheek, so to speak, and trotted off, but not without first issuing a flick of the flank that kicked poor Pim through two clubhouse walls and an estate fence, and into a pivotal role in a cricket match one field over."

"But… he punched a horse."

"In his defence," I said, "that was the first and last time."

"I daresay."

"Once every year or so he'll do something — or, perhaps more accurately, my mother will discover that he's done something — particularly scandalous, and he'll exile himself to Epping Forest to do absolution and generally stay out of her line of fright."

Diogenes wobbled by at this point. He stopped and gazed at us with that long, drawn, disappointed dewlap. Ivor held his pipe upside down to demonstrate that it was empty and the droopy dog, with a sad shake of his ears, walked on.

"What hold has your mother over Mister Pimsloe?"

"An excellent question, Inspector," I lauded. "One over which I and my kind deliberate long into winter evenings, when we know that my mother is on the continent. It's a difficult thing to convey, if you haven't met her — have you ever been before an especially obdurate magistrate who also keeps a copy of the poem you left on the pillow of the upstairs maid?"

"No."

"Well, then, it's nearly impossible to say," I resigned. "However, in the case of Uncle Pim her influence was more concrete — she had her hand constantly on the spigot."

"What spigot is that?"

"The Boisjoly bond market," I explained. "Uncle Pim, while by no means a poor man, labours for his daily bread in the capacity of trust-fund beneficiary. His monthlies come monthly, and in fixed amounts, and so his simple pastime is heavily reliant on the friendly float, particularly as the flat racing season opener at Newmarket approaches."

"And your mother can cut that off," deduced Ivor, for he is a detective.

"Can and would," I confirmed. "A word from Mama and the London credit markets would, for Uncle Pim, be closed. It's happened, too, on more than one occasion. The last time, according to family lore, Pim was compelled to sell the Bentley just to lose it all on a complicated accumulator at Epsom. My mother found out, of course, when Pim tried to turn a jockey inside out."

"Hard to believe it only happens once a year."

"Yes, it is, isn't it?" I agreed. "Frankly, Inspector, there's a broad consensus among the amateur sleuths of your acquaintance that Uncle Pim gets away with a great deal more than comes to light, through the judicious placement of the carefully calculated gratuity. There's no proof of that — and if there ever were I wouldn't put it past Mama to turn off the spigot and pour concrete down the well — but last year he touched me and uncountable other relations for a hundred pounds and, days later, his local beat bobby bought a fishing boat."

"This would have been tremendously helpful to know when I spoke to him earlier," said Ivor.

"We can speak to him again," I proposed. "He may have some insights into what happened to Doctor Smick."

"You should know, Mister Boisjoly, that I believe he does."

"Yes, I know you do, Inspector — as mentioned, Mama tells me that you've dangerously intruded on her exclusive jurisdiction as Uncle Pim's chief persecutor."

"He was heard to threaten the man," pointed out Ivor.

"He threatens everyone."

"You don't think he did it?"

"Let's ask him."

Uncle Pim's bijoux residence was a potting shed on the edge of the pond, with a weatherboard roof made mostly of gaps and a neat little terrace of mud, delineated from the surrounding wildlands by the distinction of being slightly less muddy. Uncle Pim was there, sitting on a stump and staring intently at the pond.

"What ho, chief suspect," I greeted, for he looked like he wanted bucking up.

Anyone encountering Uncle Pim's reputation prior to meeting the man himself might be forgiven for expecting something formidable, along the lines of those brick-browed blocks who linger about Limehouse where, for the price of a drink, they'll unload a ship or dispose of a body. Uncle Pim doesn't look like that. He looks more like the sort of chap who always has exact change. He's slight and small and wears it somehow aptly, as he does his bow tie and accountancy specs and brown flannel bus-riding suit.

"Shush," said Pim in a hush. "You mustn't influence them." He pointed with a nod at a pair of finches or warblers or wrens or, for all I knew, an as-yet undiscovered species of forest bird. They were having a perky little chat on a couple of water lilies, and then, without a word, one of them flew off and the other immediately followed.

"Ah ha, you see?" Pim approached the bank and pointed at the now vacant lilies. "Seven times out of ten, now, I've correctly predicted which of those starlings..." starlings, for the record,

"...would fly away first. Anty, it's a sign — you must put ten pounds each way on My Little Starling in the third at Plumpton this coming Saturday."

"Right oh."

"And don't tell your mother." Uncle Pim nudged me clubbishly. "Consider it a loan. You should put on a little something for yourself."

"Count on me, Uncular," I assured him. "With an infallible insider nod like that it can't fail. Oh, by the way, you remember Inspector Wittersham."

"Of course." Pim smiled a simple, innocent, smile, like a journeyman postman meeting his very first pomeranian. "Have you worked out what happened yet to poor Dr. Smick?"

"Yes," lied Ivor.

"No," I assured him. "We were hoping you could provide us with a little colour and context. I understand that you and he had words just before he scampered up the ladder."

"Words?" Pim wondered at this new and intriguing concept.

"Yes, words, Uncle Pim — you threatened to murder him."

"I did, Anty, that's true." Pim raised a hand to check further discussion as he watched two dragonflies skim across the surface of the pond. "I knew it," he said, as they slipped past a border of sedge grass in a photo finish. "Take note, Anty, Dragonfly in the fourth at Newbury."

"Why did you threaten Doctor Smick, Mister Pimsloe," focused Ivor.

"Somebody had to do it," said Pim. "I was nearest."

"Are you saying that everyone was angry with him?" I asked.

"Everyone, all the time," confirmed Pim. "We were having an Unladening. The man had a remarkable gift for getting up an English nose but during the Unladening it was raised to an art form."

"You saw him climb the ladder?" Ivor was referring now to his jotter and, presumably, an earlier interview with Uncle Pim. "And stay there?"

"I didn't stand guard, or anything quite of that nature, but yes, I was here, and had he come back down I would have seen him."

"And you're quite sure he didn't take anything up there with him?" I gazed in wonder at the box on the branch.

"Diogenes saw to that," said Pim. "Found a berry in his cuff. Wouldn't even let him take that up there."

"Why did you chase Doctor Smick up a tree, Uncle Pim?"

"I would prefer, Anty, if it's just the same to you," confided Uncle Pim, "to not discuss it in front of the inspector."

"I'm afraid that murder investigations are not à la carte affairs, Unks," I said. "You can have your bucolic peace far from prying police inspectors, if you want, but then you can't have any murders. It's all or nothing."

"I mean to say, just look around you, Anty." Uncle Pim gestured about us at the muddy banks of the reedy pond, the stark, spartan housing conditions, the flying insects and dense, damp wood. "He says it's all part of what he calls 'the journey' but if you ask me it's just a way to charge ten quid a day for a shack in the woods. And you wouldn't believe what passes for tea in this place."

"I might," I said. "And there's no getting the simple luxuries of home?"

"Whisky, you mean?"

"As an excellent example to hand."

"Not a single chance in a thousand," Pim estimated with a sad shake of the head. "Have you met Diogenes? He sees to all that. No whisky, no tobacco, not even tea or coffee. Do you know what they gave us for dinner last night? Consomé. And I'm not convinced it wasn't just more of that leaf tea, with a sprinkle of conifer for colour. Tasted like a lawn."

"Then why do you keep returning, Mister Pimsloe?" Ivor chewed this out from between teeth clamping an empty pipe.

"Have you ever met Mrs Boisjoly, Inspector?"

"You're in hiding?" clenched Ivor. "I find that difficult to believe."

"So, no, then," concluded Pim. "You haven't met Anty's mother. I'm maintaining a position of constructive disengagement."

"Couldn't you do that in a nice hotel?"

"Yes, well, I suppose, on balance, there may be something to be said for Doctor Smick's methods, extreme as they might be," acceded Pim. "A period at Eden Bliss Paradise allows me to collect myself."

"Then that brings us back to why it was that you threatened the doctor," navigated Ivor. "When we spoke earlier you claimed that he went to his sanctuary to do some bird watching."

"Who's to say he didn't, Inspector?" Uncle Pim straightened his bow tie. "He might have done, whether I proposed murdering him or not."

"We'll take that as read."

"You know what he did this morning? Only took away my book." Pim offered the court.

"You're not even allowed reading material?" queried Ivor.

"Not that sort of book." Pim turned his talent for straightening to his waistcoat. "An odds book. I had been making book on some of the natural wonders around us — very much getting into the spirit of things, you understand, and only for a few quid. I had a very nice little ante post going between the egg clutches of a pair of Grey Herons and two Mallard families."

"You were making book on which brood would hatch first?" marvelled Ivor.

"With a separate line offered on First Player to Score," added Pim. "Straight three-to-one because, unlike some touts I could name, I do it for the love of the sport."

"Hatchling races is a sport?"

"I also proposed a very generous line on when that dead tree is going to split and fall into the pond, and a nearest guess pool for how many times Nurse Dalimore will say the word 'uplifting' during a single Undladening." Pim gazed longingly and even lovingly at his dead tree. "Doctor Smick confiscated the book."

"And so you threatened to kill him if he didn't return it," deduced Ivor.

"No. If I'm honest, I had agreed to refrain from all forms of gambling while here." Pim's waistcoat straightening eased smoothly into button fiddling. "You might say he was within his rights. No, I'm afraid I rather lost my sang-froid. I don't understand it myself — Anty will tell you, I'm normally quite serene."

"Did you really punch a horse?"

"He had it coming."

"And how did Doctor Smick have it coming?"

"He just wouldn't let it go, would he?" Pim popped a button off his waistcoat. We watched it arc over the terrace and land in the pond. "I mean to say, of course he didn't have it coming. I confess, I may have rankled a bit when he repeatedly asked after the underlying reason why I, very rarely, kick off, a bit, when I, on occasion, lose a bet. Well, really, what sort of a question is that, I ask you? It's like asking a chap why he wants for a whisky at five o'clock."

"It's just how things are done," I seconded.

"Well, exactly."

"Did you tell him?" I asked.

"Tell him what, Anty?"

"Why it is that losing a bet as opposed to, say, losing your keys or your brolly, sends you to the peak of pique," I reminded him.

"You know perfectly well, Anty."

"I was thinking of Inspector Wittersham," I said. "He does like a good story. Don't you, Inspector, like a good story?"

"I'd like to hear this one."

"Yes, well, I'm not saying it's connected, but Doctor Smick very clearly thought it was." Uncle Pim picked his way to the water's edge and looked into it. "It's nothing, really, but I lost the love of my life on a bet."

Ivor, accustomed by my acquaintance to the instructive anecdote, withdrew a box of matches from his pocket, and even got so far as striking one before realising that he had no tobacco.

"You wagered a woman?"

"It's not as bad as it sounds," claimed Pim. "It's not as though we had an understanding. We'd only just been introduced, but my friend and clubmate, Taff Carmel, was starting from the same handicap and he, too, loved Min Baffins — the single most purely beguiling and comely girl either of us had ever met."

"The commonly accepted procedure among the rest of us, Mister Pimsloe, is to present your best case to the young lady in question, and await her decision," sniped Ivor from the depths of his tobacco dependency.

"Well, exactly so, Inspector." Uncle Pim raised an 'ah-ha' finger. "Taff looked like something carved during the Renaissance and he could play the piano and he was, well, he was like Anty, here…"

"Erudite?" I suggested. "Witty? Strangely sound on the question of the integration of Malta?"

"Skinny." Pim gazed down at his own swelling line of waistcoat buttons. "Taff had it all over me, in fact, but he was a sportsman, and so I knew my only chance of a clear final stretch to

Miss Baffins was to risk all — the loser would gracefully scratch his entry."

"How did you settle it?" asked Ivor with a tone that made the question sound more like 'why are you not confined somewhere?'

"A coin toss, as it happens," reminisced Pim with a slow shake of the head. "Taff, just like him, gave me the honour, and this is the darkest part — I chose tails."

"As sensible as any other of your choices, thus far," sniped Ivor.

"Yes, but you see, the coin was a Victoria half-crown," recounted Pim. "The barmaid who officiated was called Viccy, we were drinking Victory Blends, and we were in a pub called The Queen's Head. And I chose tails…" Pim's voice trailed off into an awed disbelief.

"I see." Ivor nodded officiously. "And Doctor Smick, by continuously reminding you of this painful experience, caused you to lose control and murder him." He turned to me and added, "It's a strong defence of mitigation. Might just keep him clear of a noose."

"I'll have to run it by Mama."

"I didn't kill Doctor Smick." Pim spoke without conviction, for he in that moment spotted his errant button. He scooped it up from the water bed. "Ha! That must mean something. Isn't there a colt named Brassy Button running this Saturday at Chelmsford?"

"You're thinking of Silver Cufflink," I reminded him, "and he's joint favourite."

Pim scowled his disappointment at the button's shortcomings as an omen.

Ivor, as it happens, was casting a similar censure on his pipe, when inspiration seemed to strike.

"Mister Pimsloe, why is it that you told Doctor Smick about your appalling wager with Mister Carmel? You must have known that he'd have pressed the point."

31

"I rather had the impression that he knew about it already." Pim adjusted his bowtie with a hunted aspect, the way a Luangwa Valley antelope, sensing a leopard on the wind, might adjust its bow tie. "Doubtless it's in that infernal file." Then he hastened to add, "There won't be anything else in there."

"What file, Uncler?"

"File?" Pim repeated the exotic new word.

"You mentioned a file," prompted Ivor.

"An infernal one, if that helps," I added.

"Oh? Oh, yes, quite. Doctor Smick kept a closed file containing the secrets of all his guests."

CHAPTER FOUR

The Stress of an Address to an Undressed Baroness

"Baroness Phyllida Garlic." Ivor referred to his jotter. "One of your lot, I take it."

Nurse Dalimore had directed us to the 'Serenity Salon' where, it was understood, we would find the aforementioned baroness.

"Not by birth, and that's really the only way we count it," I said. "Baroness Garlic was born a Caraway — solid, chorus girl stock. She performed for a while with her parents in their song and dance and cross-talk act, the Tearaway Caraways, before she married Gav Garlic, himself not much more nobly natal than the average Caraway, but for a tremendously circuitous and distant connection to the Duke of Westminster. It's now lost to the tumble of time whether it was before or after Phyllida fell irretrievably in love with Gav that she discovered that he had a tiny legacy."

"An inheritance?" presumed Ivor.

"A small one," I scaled. "Gav had grown up with the stewardship of this little strip of useless land and it never occurred to him that it might be worth anything, but Phyllida recognised it for what it was — the border between Chelsea and Kensington."

"He owned Cromwell Road?"

"The very one," I said. "Phyllida somehow managed to parlay that modest two-and-a-half-mile heirloom into a nice little stake, which she then wielded like a gilded cosh in the City capital markets and capital patriarchates to build a proper fortune and shake a baronetcy out of the palace for Gav."

We had arrived at the canvas flap of a door to the Serenity Salon, and so I lowered my voice.

"That, I hope, was all Gav ever wanted in life, because he signed off that same year."

"Natural causes?" wondered Ivor.

"In my circle, yes," I said. "A drunken disagreement with Newton's Laws of Motion. Newton was ably represented by a Bakerloo LER engine."

"I see." Ivor put his pipe in his pocket, pushed through the door of the Serenity Salon, and said, "Cor blimey!" as if I'd never heard the term properly employed until that moment. He popped back out of the tent. "Forgive me, Your Ladyship."

"Come in, Inspector," came an energetic buzz from within. "You don't think I'm coming out there like this, do you?"

"We can wait until you're done with your bath, Lady Garlic," truckled Ivor.

"It's not a bath, it's a treatment by trial, after which I'm taking my mud massage and swamp sand exfoliation. You can join me for that or we can talk now, but I don't have time in my day to do only one thing at a time. Ha!" An inspiration appeared to append that thought. "I don't have time to tell you I don't have time. You can close your eyes if you like."

We did, and pushed on through the door like two clumsy sheep trying to fit simultaneously through a stile gate.

"Afternoon, Baroness," I greeted the darkness. "Anthony Boisjoly, distant nephew in name to Pim Pimsloe."

"I know who you are, Anty," said the void. "Pim's told me all about you. The man's on the road to ruin and you're the one loaning him the money for petrol. Gambling's no way to make a fortune, young man, but it's a first-class way to lose one. Why aren't you taking notes?"

"I have an excellent recall for the obvious," I replied.

"I'm talking to the inspector."

"My eyes are closed," Ivor said as a sort of part obsequious explanation, part assertion of the strict code of honour he always brings with him into a lady's bath. Then he fumbled nervously with his matchbox, struck a match, realised once again that he had no tobacco and — from here on I'm guessing a bit — lost track of the match, which landed in my hair. I opened my eyes.

"Oh, what ho, Lady Garlic." I saw, then, that the baroness was up to her neck in a galvanised metal tub full of ice water, her head bobbing on the surface like the garnish on a garish cocktail.

The Serenity Salon was a temporary arrangement, like a rented bandstand for a village fête but with card and canvas walls, lit by natural light creeping in at a hundred points of failure in the structure. There was the tub in which the baroness was retarding her metabolism, a dressing screen, a barrel full of pine cones, a small but worrying stack of dried branches, a low fire under a steaming cauldron, and several other instruments of serenity.

Baroness Phyllida Garlic, from the neck up, was a high cheekboned, high browed, highlight with a high manner that made a chap feel rather as though he had some explaining to do.

"You can open your eyes, Inspector," I said, "Her Ladyship has a deep draught to the water line."

"Forgive the intrusion, Baroness." Inspector Wittersham has a dissonant relationship with the aristocracy — he's a firm egalitarian who comes completely unstuck in the presence of privilege. He's the modern, old-fashioned, reflective, reflexive working class mind in a working class upbringing.

"I already told you everything I saw, Inspector," said the floating head. "I know how it's supposed to work and I understand, but I'll save you a great deal of time and tell you right now that asking the same question a dozen different ways will get you nowhere with me. Directly get right to the point and I'll point you in the right direction. No, wait; asking a question again because you didn't like the answer the first time is like reading a book again because you didn't like the ending. Write that down."

"Yes, Your Ladyship."

"The inspector thought that I might be able to provide a different perspective for, as you can see, I am taller," I explained. "And he and I have form with this sort of thing."

"What sort of thing?" asked Lady Garlic from beneath an arched and incredulous brow.

"Oh, you know," I said, "impossible murders and their care, wear, and light maintenance."

"I understand from all sources that you're a wastrel, a spendthrift, a gambler, and a drunk."

"...and a drunk..." muttered Ivor as he continued to write down everything Baroness Garlic said.

"Like you, Lady Garlic, my interests are highly diversified," I explained. "That's so important in this modern economy, don't you think? Perhaps you heard reviews of our opening performance in Fray last year, involving two locked room murders and a mysterious Canterfell family codicil."

"Of course not," scorned the baroness. "The only news worth reading I don't need to read, because I made it."

Ivor nodded as he wrote that down.

"Closer to home, then, Your Ladyship," I reported, "I had a not insignificant hand in the outwardly flawless fusion of the House of Garlic, in the form of your nephew Hew, and the Binnick Family, standing for whom was Barbara, known widely and worryingly as Barbed."

"They were married in March," offhanded Lady Garlic. "It was a beautiful ceremony at Saint Botolphs, and it *was* flawless."

"I know it was — officiating was Bishop Binnock, doting uncle to Barbed and founding member of the Aldgate branch of the Temperance League. The boy's choir of Saint Dunstan's in the East performed *Der Herr denket an uns,* and Hew was punctual and perpendicular. But how different might the day have unfolded, Your Ladyship, had Hew been arrested for public drunkenness not ten hours prior to his engagement with destiny?"

"I know all about that." The baroness waved an icy hand. "He was briefly detained and found to be well within the level of inebriation expected of a young man the night before his wedding."

"In fact, he was told by a kindly police inspector that if he could walk the edge of the Serpentine without stepping once in the water, he could go home and sleep it off."

"That's correct," marvelled Garlic. "How could you possibly know that?"

"I know all, Lady Garlic," I continued. "I know, for example, that Hew was stewed to the slews. The Serpentine, as you are doubtless aware, is in Hyde Park, while the encounter with the friendly policeman occurred in the Pump Room of the Ritz Carlton. Furthermore, he believed that I was a friendly policeman."

"You?"

"I."

"I must suppose, then, that you were quite convincing."

"I was, for my own, unrelated purposes, wearing an ermine cape and antlers, Your Ladyship."

"Just a tick…" Ivor looked up from his jotter. "Antlers? What name did you give at the Ritz Carlton when you were impersonating a police inspector, Mister Boisjoly?"

"I don't believe I recall."

"I ask because it would go some distance in explaining a most peculiar letter I received from management, asking if I knew what had become of their second barman." Ivor tapped meaningfully on his jotter with his pencil.

"Terrence," I provided. "A minor settlement had to be made on the man, after which I believe he purchased a pub in Abingdon, where he has family."

"If you gentlemen are about done with this penetrating barrage of questions..." the baroness shifted like a bottle of champagne, emerging from a bucket of ice, "...I've reached optimal insensitivity."

Ivor and I turned like soldiers on parade to face the door and listen to the daring dashing of ice and water and baroness.

"We were just hoping to ask if you could confirm the circumstances under which you last saw Doctor Smick," I said.

"You can turn around, if you like." This was accompanied by what sounded like a shrubbery trying to escape.

Baroness Phyllida was behind the screen, her head peering just over the top, and as I turned she swung a leafy, spindly branch over her shoulder like a sack, absorbed the blow with a wince, and said, "Ha!"

"Lady Garlic, if I may, what is it that brings you to Eden Bliss Paradise?" I asked.

"Sometimes, Mister Boisjoly..." she struck herself a blinder over the other shoulder, "...I just need to get away and relax."

"I mean to say, what's your particular poison?" I clarified. "My understanding is that Doctor Smick's regime was designed primarily to help those who enjoy life to excess to, where possible and practicable, enjoy it less."

"Smick was a genius." The baroness found a knot on the branch that she liked and smacked it against what appeared a tender spot on her spine. "He could read people the way I can read the City financial markets — not so well, obviously, but perfection is almost always a surplus when excellence will suffice." She gave herself another slap with the branch, and then another, and fell into a rhythm. "He identified the weakness..." Paff! "...then the root of the weakness..." Waff! "...then the treatment and that!..." Baff!

"...that is the genius of the method — people will always pay for a cure, if you give them the disease for free. Ha!" She gave herself a congratulatory paff on the back. "Write that down."

"And what vice takes ice?" I asked.

"I have no interest in the ailment," thwacked the baroness. "I just want the treatment. The doctor and I were going to take the Smick System national... international! There'll be Eden Bliss Paradise Health Resorts anywhere there's excess — we were planning three just for Belgium."

"You and the doctor had a business relationship, Your Ladyship?" Ivor asked his jotter.

"Of a sort. He had no relationship with business and I have no business with relationships, but I saw the potential that he failed to see."

"Is that still proceeding?" I asked.

"I don't see why it shouldn't." The baroness ceased striking herself with shrubbery to reflect on this. "We had an agreement, and I know enough now about the system to reproduce it."

"If you had no need of Eden Bliss Paradise yourself, Baroness, how do you come to know Doctor Smick?" I averted my eyes with casual cause to Ivor's notepad. He was writing 'agreement?'

"I've known him for years." The baroness discarded her branch and took up a robe from the top of the screen. "We go back to the music hall days, when he called himself The Amazing Professor Smick. He had a mind-reading act."

"One of those chaps who calls out 'I'm seeing a... Bill, is it? Is there a Bill in the audience, or someone who knows a Bill?'" I guessed. "I once saw The Marvellous Mesmo at the Palladium tell the audience that he was detecting a 'Woodrow, known to the police as Sticky Mickey.' Fully three chaps jumped up and ran out of the theatre."

"Smick was an expert cold reader." Baroness Garlic came out from behind her screen and Ivor exhaled a gale of relief on seeing that she was wearing a neck-to-deck bathrobe. "He also did a hypnosis bit."

"That must have been more difficult to blag out," I supposed.

"My father was his shill," explained Lady Phyllida. "One of the great music hall stooges. Every night he'd reluctantly get pulled on stage and claim to be 'Barry from Birmingham' and then, on command, act like a chicken or as though he believed his hands were made of lead."

"It was planned in advance?" I marvelled.

"Every evening, before each show, The Amazing Professor Smick would dictate to my father every detail, including how the cigarette girls should pretend to faint, when appropriate."

"You're not suggesting that The Marvellous Mesmo is fake," I put to her. "At that very same show, I'll have you know, he had a chap, under hypnosis, confess to starting the Great Fire of London. Then a policeman came out and hit him over the head with a rubber mallet. It was all very dramatic."

"Papa was a deep-dyed professional." The proud showman's daughter raised a 'now mark you' finger. "Although, one day he spotted the casting director for *As You Were* in the audience, and instead of clucking like a chicken he did the soliloquy from Hamlet."

"A not insignificant departure," I observed. "I've seen both."

"Doctor Smick always felt I owed him something for that, which is why, when he developed his method by curing himself of a thirty-cigarette-a-day habit, he came to me for financing for his health resort," recalled the baroness. "I'm glad I didn't follow my first instincts and kick him down the stairs. Ha! Never follow first instincts, but keep them on hand, you're sure to find a use for them. No, wait — always take a moment for calm reflection, then act on impulse. Write that down."

"Yes, Baroness." Ivor scratched both aphorisms into his jotter, just to be safe. "Returning to the last time you saw the doctor…"

"I believe I told you all that already, Inspector." The baroness dipped a ladle into the steaming cauldron.

"For Mister Boisjoly's benefit, if you please, Your Ladyship."

The baroness withdrew the ladle and with it a towel, which she wrapped around her head, leaving a small gap through which to speak. She lay on a bamboo chaise longue.

"Very well, I can indulge you for as long as the steam lasts." The towel was emitting what looked a durable mist. "We were having an Unladening. I believe the doctor was asking your uncle what it was he'd been getting up to in London since his last visit. Pim asked the doctor what business it was of his, and the doctor said that during the Unladening such things were everybody's business, and Pim offered to unladen the doctor's head from his shoulders, or words to that general effect. I recall that this proposal was met with broad approval and the doctor prescribed himself a short period of reflection in his sanctuary. We all dispersed, then, so we were outside when Smick was checked by Diogenes, who found a berry or something before letting him climb up. He never came back down. Some time later he called out something about being poisoned."

"And no one else went up?" asked Ivor.

"Nobody could have," muffled the baroness. "He pulled the ladder up, and you've seen the sanctuary — it's in the middle of the compound. Anyone climbing up there would have been seen."

"Did I understand you, Baroness, to say that everyone at the Unladening agreed with the general principle, as outlined by my uncle, that Doctor Smick's head should be pulled off?"

"Everyone apart from myself," specified the baroness. "Yes."

"And is it also your understanding that some of this animosity might come from files that the doctor ostensibly kept on all his patients?" I wondered.

"Not about me," claimed Lady Garlic. "All he had in those files about me was our agreement, duly signed. But for everyone else, it was astonishing some of the things that he knew. You want to know how to avoid scandal, Anty? Be so poor that no one cares or so rich that you don't. Ha! Write that down."

CHAPTER FIVE

The Pomeranian's Peculiar Position Pertaining to the Postman

"Did you really write all that down?"

Ivor reviewed his notes as we walked across the muddy compound.

"Rather a lot of it, yes." He turned numerous pages of his telegraph jotter in a sort of daze. "It just seemed the safest course of action."

"Who's next?"

"Ehm…" Ivor reversed several pages. "Sir Melvin Otterwater."

The route took us across the compound and as we approached the poisoning tree — an arthritic, dead oak that arched this way then that to form a building foundation of impossible physics — a neglected question came back to me.

"Where's the body?"

"In the Smoking Lounge." Ivor pointed with his pipe at a hewn-stone hovel.

"There's a smoking lounge?"

"No," murmured Ivor with menace. "There isn't. It's called that for therapeutic reasons, I understand. Everyone gathers there after meals and during the cocktail hour for a minimum of half an hour of not smoking. It's also the coldest building, so that's where the coroner set up."

"The coroner is already here?"

"I brought him along with me." Ivor nodded resentfully at the Smoking Lounge.

"And how did you manage to get the body down from the treehouse?"

"Largely independently." Ivor spoke with the tone of a persecuted man who just wants to smoke his pipe. "In the end, I had to lower the poor chap by rope. Babbage was waiting on the ground."

"Mister Babbage is still a coroner?" I knew from a previous encounter that Mister Babbage's fondest ambition was to sell the post of County Coroner and retire to a life of mangling wurzels.

"He has been unable to sell the post, what with the new requirement that coroners be, in some fashion, qualified for the job."

I recalled a coroner of generous physique who wouldn't have been harmed in the slightest by a short course of treatment at Eden Bliss Paradise Health Resort. Or even a long one. "He never carried a body."

"He supervised." Ivor's rarely mistakeable irony was herein abraded by abstinence to a blunt instrument. "Then I had to climb down and take the feet while the other gentlemen guests took the shoulders in shifts of two yards a turn. Took us a good hour to do what, if even you'd been here, should have been five minutes. At least that dog made Babbage turn over his cigars."

From his upended rain barrel dog house, Diogenes watched this conversation unfold. With a sigh, he rolled to his feet and approached, jouncing from side to side on his stubby legs, his elongated beagle-liveried snout sagging and sad and prepared for any and all and only disappointment. He huffed to the base of the tree and then sat, his head tilted judgmentally, his eyes glistening with unshed tears for the human condition, his entire demeanour a map of quiet despair for the overleaping failings of the human race. He presented as though, but for the sustaining hope of one day meeting the world's one honest man, he'd gladly lay down and die.

"We're only passing through," I explained to the dog. "You couldn't direct us to Sir Melvin Otterwater, could you?"

Diogenes shook his head slowly and sadly, waddled closer, looked up at me and, and said "Woof," in a tired melancholy.

"I swear to you, Diog old dog, I left everything in the care of Vickers."

He just stared at me, though. He stared through me, more accurately, and saw there something that typically only my mother could see.

"You quite sure you're not carrying anything, Boisjoly?" asked Ivor, clearly choosing sides.

"Quite…" Then I saw in the dog's drooping eyes the dreadful truth. "Op," I conceded, and bent and raised my right trouser leg, exposing the ankle flask I'd attached that morning and forgotten, in light of the generous hospitality offered by the bar car of the Liverpool Street to Epping omnibus service. "Sorry about that, Diogenes — I shall dispose of this immediately." Reproached, I quickly drained the flask. "There we go."

"You don't have any tobacco down there, by any chance," wondered Ivor.

"I do not."

"What a remarkable animal." Ivor watched Diogenes turn a despondent tail and stamp away towards the tree line.

"It's in practice a sixth sense. A basset hound can detect with a sniff of a still wind what you can with both eyes and a formal inquest. In fact, chap at my club…"

"Please don't, Mister Boisjoly."

"You'll like this one, Inspector," I claimed. "It's got a dog in it."

"And it's somehow relevant to the investigation?"

"Not in the slightest," I assured him. "You see, this chap at my club, Links Fairgreen, had a basset hound that could talk."

"No, he didn't."

"No, you're right, he didn't," I conceded. "But Links was convinced that Bags — the dog's name was, in fact, Baguette, with dual reference to the national origins and general design of the breed — was spying on him, and reporting his activities to Mrs Fairgreen."

"Why did he think that?"

"Because that's exactly what was happening." I kept pace with Ivor as we followed Diogenes' doggy tracks. "Links enjoyed taking Bags for long walks, particularly when his wife's mother was visiting, and would often combine this passion with one or two others, such as practising his short game on the Heath, testing his luck at an innocent but technically illegal casino on a barge permanently docked at Camden Lock, or exchanging tips and quips with other ardent dog-walkers at the Cricketers on the Green."

"And the dog objected to this?" Ivor spoke idly as he watched Diogenes describe a sentry path along the treeline.

"By all appearances Baguette was happy with the arrangement. He didn't even need a lead. He would patter along next to Links doing what all basset hounds do the world over — charting physical reality with his nose to the ground, learning, recording, interpreting, analysing, and mapping world and welkin through that precision nasute. Mrs Links, on the other hand, while not explicitly outlawing putting, gambling, and drinking during her mother's frequent visits, tacked rather towards tender disapproval and the sad, slow, turn away that deftly and dolefully says, 'I expected so much better.' Links said that it was worse than missing a two-footer on a tied hole."

"How does the dog enter into it, then?" Ivor asked as, in that moment, Diogenes disappeared into the woods.

"It became clear that despite Links' best efforts, Mrs Links always knew what he was up to," I explained. "They'd come back from their walk, and Mrs Links would dote over Baguette and whisper in his ear. Links initially took this for the inexplicable babble that reflexively comes to certain people in the presence of adorable animals, and the huffing and woofing with which Baguette replied his way of politely acknowledging it."

"Which it obviously was."

"And yet," I continued, "the moment after communing with Bags, Mrs Links would take on that sad bunny expression and say something like 'I do wish you wouldn't take Baguette to the Heath — there are foxes.'"

"Doubtless the animal's feet were wet."

"Or, 'If you must take Baguette to the pub I wish you'd at least sit in the garden — he's very sensitive to tobacco smoke.'"

Ivor reflexively withdrew his pipe from his pocket and in that same moment Diogenes' immense snout pushed through a blackthorn bush and, in a spiritual, canine way, sighed. Ivor put his pipe back in his pocket.

"And this is what convinced Links that he had a talking dog."

"No, Cores Pommeroy convinced him that he had a talking dog."

"Who is Cores Pommeroy?" withered Ivor. "Or is that pertinent? Feel free to assume that it isn't."

"Cores Pommery — the chap with the pomeranian who attacks postmen." I reminded him, before recalling, "Oh, that's right, that was Nurse Dalimore. We'll return to Cores later, if it's convenient, Inspector — we have a murder investigation to conduct. It's sufficient to know that Cores was acquainted with a pomeranian called Nibbleit, who would attack the postman."

"Noted."

47

"And in an effort to address the problem of unreliable mail service, Cores took Nibbleit to see a specialist — a blue-haired boffin calling herself Madame A. Boyer and claiming that she could communicate with dogs and horses, in all cases, and certain breeds of cat, if they felt like talking."

"You're not going to tell me this charlatan cured Nibbleit of biting the postman," doubted Ivor.

"No, but Cores was impressed by her abilities all the same. She was unable to convince Nibbleit to adopt a live-and-let-live attitude towards the postal service, but she was at least able to identify the root cause of the problem — turns out that Nibbleit just really hates postmen."

"I see."

"Thinks of them as smug and officious, apparently." I raised my swear-by hand. "Her words, not mine."

Ivor, who had been once again scanning the woods, spared a moment to settle upon me a fatigued expression.

"Cores, as I say, was convinced," I continued. "And he in turn persuaded Links to engage Madame Boyer as his lead negotiator."

"Negotiator?" Ivor humoured me distractedly as he discreetly withdrew his pipe and held the bowl to his nose and inhaled the charred perfume of wistful history.

"Links wanted to know what else Baguette had told the wife, and if there was an arrangement by which he might exercise some influence over that which was said to Mrs Links in future, thus turning a current liability into a reliable channel of misinformation."

"I take it that the strategy failed." Ivor was now affectionately scraping his pipe with a dottle pick.

"Not by first appearances, no," I recounted. "According to Links, he was witness to a lengthy conversation between Madame Boyer and Baguette, along the lines of 'Bow wow?', 'Bow wow wow,' 'Woof?', 'Woof woof, *woof,*' 'Wooooof,' 'Woof,' and so on in that vein, and eventually, switching to English, she told Links that contrary to appearances, the basset hound didn't enjoy long, muddy walks through London, and would be willing to provide Mrs Links with consistent reports of pleasant outings in the park, if in future they could travel by taxi."

"The dog wanted to ride in a taxi." Ivor held his pipe up to the light, for some reason, and admired it with one eye closed.

"According to Madame Boyer, yes, and for several weeks the agreement, by all appearances, held, until one day on returning from a particularly foul streak of overdraws at the clandestine Camden casino, Mrs Links communed with Baguette as usual and then said, 'I do wish you wouldn't spend so much on taxis, Links, particularly when the whole idea is to give you and Baguette some exercise.'"

"The dog broke the agreement?" Ivor appeared to ask his pipe.

"Links saw it as not only a flagrant violation of the treaty, but something of a final straw in a baleful evening," I recounted. "He saw no value in restraint, and he told his wife all — the putting practice, the Cricketers, the not insubstantial gambling losses and, perhaps above all, his dislike of his mother-in-law. After all, he reasoned, Mrs Links had already learned most of it from the dog, she might as well hear his side of the story."

"But she did not, it came to pass, already know," divined, somehow, Ivor.

"The best stories practically tell themselves, don't they?" I said. "She did not, and to this day Links has been walking the dog and being solicitous to the mother-in-law and abstaining from the pub, the casino, and even the golf course, in an effort to undo the damage."

"Well?"

"Well what? Inspector?"

"How did Mrs Fairgreen know where Links had been and that he'd been riding in taxis?"

"By examining Baguette's ears," I replied. "In addition to a pronounced proboscis, basset hounds are famous for their comically long lobes, and when combined to comb the surface of the world, the ears collect mud from the park, stagnant water from the lock, and sawdust from the floor of the pub."

At that moment, the door of the Smoking Lounge opened with a burst and Mister Babbage, county coroner, stalked through as though driven by proud purpose. Babbage doesn't carry purpose well, though — he's a roundish sort of bloke and he tends to compound the impression with round effects; he wears a bowler hat over his halo of white hair, round-gorged suits, a bow tie, and an all-round character of dissatisfaction with the quality of strangers, colleagues, and friends.

"What ho, Mister Babbage," I hailed.

He stopped, squinted hard at me for a moment, and then approached us with, if possible, more pronounced purpose.

"Have you got any cigars?" Optimistically, he held out a hand.

"I don't, I'm afraid."

The coroner sighed eloquently, clearly expressing that he expected as much from the likes of me.

"Give me a cigarette, then."

"Again, you catch me at a moment when I'm unable to accommodate," I pleaded.

"Then might I enquire, sir, by what infernal neck you interrupted my walk to the nearest tobacconist?"

"You can't walk to Epping, Mister Babbage," I assured him.

"I can and will crawl to Epping, yoked to a coal wagon, if that's where I'll find a cigar," vowed Babbage. "Do you know of one closer?"

"In a very real manner of speaking, I do, Mister Babbage," I happily reported. "My man, Vickers, will be returning shortly with

Mister Livesy and his giant horse, and if we complete the investigation by then, you might return with him."

Babbage addressed the inspector, "I thought it was all sorted."

"Mister Boisjoly has some doubts about his uncle's guilt," said Ivor.

Babbage snatched his bowler from his head and regarded it as though wondering if it could be smoked. "Smick pulled the ladder up after him. He clearly felt his life was in danger. Charge this Pimsloe chap with murder and we can go back to civilisation."

"Well, exactly," I said. "He pulled up the ladder. No one, perhaps particularly Uncle Pim, could have climbed up to kill him, and he took nothing with him. Didn't you tell me, Inspector, that all of the men had difficulty carrying even their share of the body for more than a few yards? Could any of them have climbed that tree?"

"Pimsloe threatened to kill the man, didn't he?" Babbage screwed the hat back on his head, freeing his hands for anxious wringing.

"It appears that there may be others who had cause to resent Doctor Smick," said Ivor. "Did you find any keys on the body? It would probably be of the smaller sort, such as for a filing cabinet."

"Do you mean this one?" Babbage withdrew a key from his pocket. "The tag reads 'filing cabinet'."

"That may very well be the one," I ventured.

"Have you had hold of this key since the body was brought down?" asked Ivor.

"It was in his pocket." Babbage passed the key to the inspector. "And little else. That key, a wallet — no cigars, no cigarettes, not so much as a pinch of snuff."

"He has been described as inconsiderate," I said.

"And no one could have had access to this key, for example the men who helped carry the body to the Smoking Lounge," pressed Ivor.

"If there's anything a man wanting of a cigar likes more it's to be made to answer the same question on regular rotation." Once again Babbage removed his bowler, punched it, and put it back on. Then he bit his thumb. "When is Livesy getting back, did you say?"

"I very neatly avoided giving a precise estimate, Mister Babbage," I confessed. "My private objective was to provide you hope while we completed the investigation."

"I've already done my bit," claimed Babbage. "I can only tell you how the man was killed. You can work out who did it."

"A fast-acting poison," I repeated for context. "But we still don't know how it was delivered."

"You don't," said Babbage, "but I do."

"I have an idea, Mister Babbage — why not tell us" I proposed. "Just in case something happens to you, you understand."

"You can see for yourself." Babbage turned with the energy and agility of a man denied a pressing addiction, and led us back to the Smoking Lounge.

I had an immediate insight into the mind of the stymied smoker. The Smoking Lounge was a deliberately uncomfortable, cold, stone room of iron furniture and uneven walls of overlapping advertising. The posters were, predictably in hindsight, for cigarettes. There were happy, blithe flappers riding motorboats with long, thin Sciggaratti between their ruby lips, gruff, rough cowboys gazing across the Arizona desert through the smoke of a thick, tarry Gladstone, society wags in tuxedos and ball gowns sharing the atmosphere of dozens of Black Velvets in long cigarette holders. There were also advertisements featuring fishermen smoking pipes and gentlemen smoking cigars, obviously, and standing ashtrays dotted about the room. Ivor and Babbage both visibly shuddered.

"I understand it's meant to make you face your temptations in an environment in which you can't possibly succumb to them," explained Ivor with a dark resentment.

"I've seen many depraved, soulless atrocities in my line..." Babbage shook his head at what he saw about him, like a missionary stumbling into an ancient temple specialising in human sacrifice and a subsidiary line in drowning puppies. "...never have I seen anything this inhumane."

"You claim you know how the poison was delivered, Mister Babbage." Ivor drummed his pipe against the palm of his hand.

"I don't make claims, Inspector." Babbage beat his hat against his hip. "Have a look for yourself."

Babbage made reference to an entity, covered in a waterproof tarpaulin, on a glass countertop which, I realised in the moment, was surplus from a tobacconist shop.

"If you would kindly just explain, if you please, Mister Babbage." Ivor put his pipe in his pocket, took it back out, and then put it back. And then took it out again.

We approached the cigar display and Babbage drew back the canvas, revealing a very calm and composed Doctor Smick.

"There," said Babbage, with meaning.

"Where?" I asked.

"There, just there." Babbage pointed at Smick's neck. "It's this habit young people these days have picked of not smoking," Babbage confided to Ivor. "It weakens the eyesight."

Ivor and I leaned in and, in fact, didn't need to, for Babbage was right. A large, round, perfect puncture was evident on the victim's neck.

Babbage dropped the tarpaulin and gave his verdict.

"Poison dart."

CHAPTER SIX

The Thinner and the Broader of Sir Melvin Otterwater

"Would you have taken note of a poison dart at the scene, Inspector?"

Ivor and I were in the compound, having left Mister Babbage gazing with damp eyes at a selection of enlargements from the pages of the illustrated catalogue of *Hija de Cabañas y Carbajal.*

Ivor considered my question carefully before saying, "You're asking if I might have overlooked a poison dart at the scene of a murder."

"Well, you might have thought it was a bird," I suggested. "Or a shoe horn."

"A shoe horn."

"I'm trying to provide you a graceful exit."

"There was no poison dart in Doctor Smick nor in the sanctuary," insisted Ivor. "It must have been removed, if it was ever there."

"Mister Babbage seemed quite convinced." We had left the coroner in the Smoking Lounge and were once again proceeding across the compound to our next interview. "If Doctor Smick was indeed, as Mister Babbage contends, sent through the mortal portal by a heavy dose of a strong poison, and with no other way of getting it into his system apart from a not insubstantial hole above his left shoulder, we're left with a different impossible mystery..."

"...what happened to the murder weapon," Ivor completed for me, as the best team mates will often do.

"Shall we first consider the matter of the ample Sir Melvin Otterwater?" I proposed.

"Is he very ample?" wondered Ivor.

"You've met the man," I confessed, "while I have not, but his proportions are famous. I'm in no position to confirm nor deny, but his tailor, I understand, received his royal warrant on Sir Melvin's recommendation."

"For uniforms?"

"Sails."

"I'm not certain this is the same chap."

"There's only one Sir Melvin Otterwater in the kingdom, Inspector," I assured him. "And I don't mean to suggest that he tends to the fuller habit, but he once won his weight in potatoes at a church fund-raiser in Knebbly-upon-Stomp, sold the lot and bought a Rover 9/20."

"We all have our weaknesses, Mister Boisjoly." Ivor held his pipe and looked to the horizon.

"Of course," I agreed. "Like poor Erysichthon of Thessaly."

"Chap from your club?"

"No, you're probably thinking of Dewey Mildenhall."

"No."

"Champers Monfoy?"

"Who is this Eric of Thornhill?" said Ivor, and I made a mental note to resolve the matter at a later date.

"Erysichthon of Thessaly," I corrected. "A prince of Thessaly, in ancient Greece. You'd probably know the area better as Aeolia, as it's called in the Odyssey."

Ivor regarded me beneath hooded eyes. He seemed to require fuller knowledge, which I provided, "It seems, for reasons which differ from account to account, Erysich wanted a goodly portion of the forest cleared, but his woodcutters stopped when they came to a sacred oak, ornamented with tributes to the goddess Demeter who, in addition to managing the cycle of growth and harvest, liked her tributes. Kept her in touch with her public."

Ivor, spotting some promising sign at the treeline, set off.

"The woodcutters refused to chop down Demeter's oak tree, so the prince took an axe and did it himself," I continued as I jogged alongside, "in so doing, he also gave a wood nymph a fatal case of decapitation — you can see where this is going."

"Can I?"

"Demeter regarded many wood nymphs among her closest friends and confidants," I explained. "Much like the warm regard you and I share, if that helps put the matter in perspective."

"Is that smoke?" Ivor squinted into the dense woods before setting off at a loping gallop.

"Demeter got her friend Limos to visit upon Erysichthon one of those hideous, insidious punishments they were always improvising."

"Which was?" Ivor reached the tree line and we could see that there was, in fact, smoke coming from somewhere.

"Insatiable hunger," I replied. "Erysichthon of Thessaly would never again know the satisfaction of a good meal well bolted. The more he ate, the hungrier he became. He sold all his possessions and even his daughter to buy food, but all he ever hence ate served only as appetisers."

"And the point, if there is one, Mister Boisjoly?" Ivor said this as the only slightly more diplomatic alternative to just growling.

"That our addictions are often out of our control," I answered. "Or, watch where you swing your axe. I suppose it could be both."

"Just a minute..." Ivor ceased his pursuit of the smoke to gain his bearings and scoff at my story. "...this is all Greek mythology? Not a story about a chap at your club — not an uncle or a cousin?"

"Well, as it happens, Inspector, the tale does put one in mind of Vats Swillingdon," I acknowledged. "Vats *is* a chap at my club and, like Erysichthon of Thessaly, eating only serves to increase his appetite, except instead of eating food it's drinking whisky. Uncanny, though, isn't it?"

At that moment Ivor and I broke through the foliage into a small, calm nave, carpeted with pine needles and screened by reaching firs which formed and filtered the waning daylight as though through stained glass. Straining the illusion of the divine was a cheerful, cherubic chap sitting on a log and tending a tiny but tremendously smoky fire.

"Sir Melvin Otterwater," spotted Ivor. "May I introduce Anthony Boisjoly."

"Or just Anty, if you fear formality coming between us, Sir Melvin."

Sir Melvin Otterwater smiled through the smoke and declared himself honoured, and then returned to poking his fire with a branch. He was a comfortably cushiony model of chap but not, as his reputation widely and roundly would have it, immense. He seemed a rather reduced sort of knight of the realm, in fact, like rhubarb coulis, and his suit looked as though it had been inherited from his bigger brother upon said bigger brother being slain by David. His earth-toned tweeds flapped about him as though they were meant to have gone round twice more, and his collar lolled like a horseshoe on a peg.

"I think we have a mutual acquaintance, sir Melvin." Ivor and I took the liberty of a seat on a log across from the subject.

"Yes." Melvin held up his smoking stoke-stick. "I know your uncle, Postlewick Pimsloe."

"I was referring to Carnaby, head steward of the Juniper Gentlemen's Club," I said. "He tells me that you outbid him when he went to Claridge's to collect our Shrove Tuesday pastries."

"Was that your man?" Melvin looked up into a wistful past somewhere in the trees. "You must express my apologies. I was in a frenzy of hunger. Doubtless I was overly expressive."

"You threatened to eat him," I reminded him. "But Carnaby is the finest steward of the finest club in London — he's heard much worse. If anything, he was more offended by your offer of a hundred pounds to walk away."

"It was all I could spare."

"I mean that you made the offer at all," I clarified. "The man has an unshakeable sense of duty, and fully two dozen Junipers went without breakfast pastries. We had to make do with roast beef and champagne."

"I say, I am sorry. I hadn't eaten for hours."

"Think nothing of it, Sir Melvin." I waved my absolution hand. "Purely out of curiosity, though, what happened to all the marsepane?"

"It was a bank holiday," said Melvin, with the tone of a man stating the obvious. "I needed *something* for later in the day."

As he'd been speaking, Sir Melvin was constructing a clever tripod out of green spruce branches, and now he employed it to suspend a tin pot over the fire.

"Could you tell us again what you recall of the events earlier today, Sir Mevlin?" Ivor spoke with authority but he was gazing at the smoke with something akin to childlike wonder.

"Certainly, Inspector." Sir Melvin reached into the bulky pockets of his coat — exactly the kind of overstuffed pockets that a chipmunk would have if chipmunks wore suits with pockets — and withdrew handfuls of what looked to be debris. "It was directly after the Unladening — I say directly after, in fact we didn't finish the session before Doctor Smick elected to retire to his sanctuary."

"And this was in direct response to threats from Mister Pimsloe, is that correct?" Ivor positioned himself in the path of the smoke and inhaled deeply.

"Certainly it coincided with that," Sir Melvin examined a chestnut, discarded it, and examined another, "but there was a general feeling of animosity. Sentiments can run rather high and prickly during the Unladenings and the Avower Hour and Cocktail Time in the Smoking Lounge. Especially Cocktail Time, now I think of it."

"Do you mean to say that everyone was irate with Doctor Smick?" I asked.

"Oh, yes, everyone." Sir Melvin reflected on his chestnut. "I think that might have been rather the point."

"Including, just as a random control subject, Baroness Garlic?"

"She tried to stab him with a high-heeled shoe."

"And yourself, Sir Melvin?"

He looked down. "I'm wearing walking boots."

"And very handsome they are, Sir Melvin," I said. "Were you among the incensed?"

"I'm not much of a joiner, if I'm honest," Sir Melvin dropped two select chestnuts — the upper band of a narrow field, from where I sat — into the pot, "but I supported the majority view."

"And you hold that he couldn't have taken anything with him when he went up the ladder?" Ivor spoke from within a cloud of campfire smoke.

"Oh, yes." Melvin now pulled a handful of acorns from his pocket. "He'd hardly have had time to pack anything, even if it weren't for Diogenes standing guard." He tested an acorn between his teeth. "That dog made me surrender my emergency ration of basil."

Sir Melvin added several acorns to the pot with what I suspect was a casual disregard for the original recipe, and then he withdrew a handful of mushrooms from the other pocket. Ivor emerged from the fumes, coughing and with tears in his eyes and appearing, in the main, dissatisfied with the smoke from a windfall fire as a tobacco substitute.

"Are those from the forest, Sir Melvin?"

"They are." Melvin sniffed the mushrooms, one by one, and dropped them into the pot. "They're quite abundant, but they have a slightly musty finish, I think, not unlike the Risotto Pavese at Pinoli's, with just a hint of leaky cellar."

"Should you be eating those?" asked Ivor. "They could be poisonous."

"They're not." Melvin dropped in the last of the mushrooms and returned to stoking the fire. "There are no poisonous mushrooms in Epping Forest."

"You can't know that."

"Oh, but I can, Inspector." The chef nodded earnestly at the Inspector. "I've tried them all. Also every leaf, root, berry and bark." He turned back to his stew. "And most of the insects."

"And none of them are poisonous?" doubted Ivor.

Melvin glanced skyward. "I recall wishing that the dogwood berries had done me in, but no, particularly not at this time of year. And there's never anything that could kill instantly, if that's what you're thinking."

"It was, yes." Ivor watched the smoke longingly. "Is there anything that passes for tobacco?"

"Crushed, dried pine cones," replied Sir Melvin without pause. "It's an excellent deterrent. Lord Snowsill-Willit was up here last summer. Doctor Smick had him on an hourly course of pine cone cigars. Gave up a twenty-five-year habit in a weekend."

"Do you come up every year yourself?" I asked.

"Oh, no, of course not," scoffed Sir Melvin. "Every two months or so. It's been six weeks since my last cure."

"But, you look quite svelte and feline," I observed. "Just in for a tuneup?"

"That's Doctor Smick's doing." Sir Melvin opened his coat and looked down at the scarcity of Sir Melvin. "I can't help myself, when I'm back in London." He caught my eye with snap urgency. "Anty, have you ever had *les aspics de gibier* at Chez Jules? They serve it with broken new potatoes fried in goose fat…" Here his voice cracked and he looked away.

"I have," I enthused. "But have you had their *sole meuniere?* It comes with an anchovy and spinach *puré* stewed in butter and garlic."

"Divine." Sir Melvin placed his palms together and raised his eyes skyward, then lowered them to hold me in frank regard. "Though Dover Sole can be a mite smallish, this time of year. I had to have three of them last time."

"In one sitting?"

"And some cake." Melvin nodded guilelessly. "I say 'some' — I had a cake."

"Have Chez Jules the sort of pastry chef that does cake?" I wondered.

"I brought my own."

"You brought your own cake to a French restaurant?" I marvelled.

"I brought my own pastry chef," clarified Melvin. "Speaking of which, Anty, the profiteroles that Claridge's serves at Sunday brunch…"

"Rum," I anticipated. "They put Bermudian rum in the custard."

"Of course."

"Oh, I say, how long have you been here this time, Sir Melvin?"

"A fortnight, two days, one breakfast, one lunch, and a teatime."

"Then you won't know that Claridge's have acquired the pastry chef from Maxim's."

"Antoine Francoeur?" inhaled Melvin. "In London?"

"Last Saturday night was his debut performance," I reported. "Individual *mille-feuilles,* infused with chocolate and raspberry on alternating layers, and drizzled with reduction of sweet coffee."

Melvin didn't answer. He just put a hand to his mouth and shook his head and made a sort of 'eep' sound.

Finally he closed his eyes and summoned from somewhere an ethereal calm. The fire crackled. An acorn popped out of the pot. Somewhere a bird said something to another bird.

"Inspector..." announced Sir Melvin. "I have business in the city."

"Just one more point, if you please, Sir Melvin." Ivor toyed idly with a pine cone with the toe of his shoe. "Are you aware of the existence of any secret files in the possession of Doctor Smick?"

Sir Melvin opened his eyes. "Secret files? No, they were no secret."

"You've seen them, then?" asked Ivor.

"Oh, you mean secret in that sense." Melvin withdrew from the folds a fork, pencil, and notepad. "No, I haven't seen them, but I know they exist. Everyone does." With the fork, he plucked a mushroom from the pot and popped it into his mouth, nodding thoughtfully as he chewed. He swallowed and wrote something short in his notepad, which he interpreted to me, as a fellow searcher of knowledge, as "Two stars, I think."

"Out of?"

"Five," said Melvin, as he plucked a hot chestnut from the pot. "From repellant to barely edible."

"What about that which you find pleasing to the palate?" I asked.

"The question has yet to arise." Melvin chewed the chestnut in intense reflection, then held his nose and closed his eyes and swallowed. Then he gave the chestnut three stars.

"Sir Melvin, if you please," insisted Ivor. "What is in these files?"

"In my case, the doctor had detailed proof that I was not complying with the regime to which we agreed when I was last here." Melvin turned to confide in me, "And I don't regret a morsel. My first day back was carvery day at Barribault's. I had them wheel the entire roast beef cart over to my table and leave it there."

"And the others?" persisted Ivor.

"Lamb, I think, and pheasant."

"I'm referring to the files Doctor Smick had on the other guests." Ivor once again produced his pipe and appeared to just pose with it. "What was in the files about the other guests of Eden Bliss Paradise?"

"Oh, I couldn't say, Inspector," said Sir Melvin. "But he knew everybody's secrets."

CHAPTER SEVEN

The Name of the Game is Gaming the Name

"Henrietta Hackenit," inventoried Ivor. "She's in the games room."

"There's a games room?"

"You'll see," said Ivor with what was, for him, a cryptic nod, and led back through the brush towards the prison camp.

"Well?" welled Ivor along the way. "What are you going to tell me about Miss Hackenit?"

"Not a thing," I said. "I've never met nor heard of the woman. Why? Does she seem my sort?"

"Not in the slightest." Ivor pushed through into the compound. "Seems quite respectable, in fact."

She did, in fact. Henrietta Hackenit had what would turn out to be a deceptively middle-school-mistress quality about her, or a vicar's wife. When we found her in the games room, leaning over the snooker table, she had about her a vaguely hunted air, like that same vicar's wife tracked to a smugglers' bar in Lisbon where she'd already traded the church roof fund for passage to Singapore.

If she had a dark side — and it would soon turn out that she did — she hid it well behind a pinafore dress and blousy buttony blouse that appeared to be made out of doilies. Her hair was bunned up and she presented a simple, unpainted countenance and looked as though she ought to be covered in cat hair.

Ivor made the introductions, "Miss Hackenit, this is…"

"Why, hello, Anty." Henrietta Hackenit peeled herself off the snooker table and leaned on her cue and smiled at me like an old friend come to pay a debt.

64

"Enchanted, Miss Hackenit," I said. "I take it my uncle gave advance warning of my arrival."

"He did," Henrietta assured me. "Call me Henrietta. Or just Henny. Or Hen, if you're easily amused. You probably don't recall, but that's what you called me last boat race night. Mind you, you were a bit in your cups — you also called me Freddy, Teddy, Your Grace, and something in French."

"I am sorry," I said, juggling recollections. "That does sound like something I'd do."

"Not a bit of it," Henny reassured me. "I was ninety proof myself. It's possible and even probable that I introduced myself under an assumed name. It's wise practice at the beginning of boat race night and other special occasions of that sort — Saturdays, for instance — to pick one false name and remember it. The difficulty, I find, is in remembering wise practice."

Henrietta had turned back to the table at this point and completed her shot, which went wild. Her cue, I noticed, was bent, and the table, for that matter, was not a parallelogram. More of a rhombus, or whatever name geometry gives to a shape of four unequal sides, one of which is slightly curved. The whole games room — which was an adjunct to the dining hall and both were low, earth and fenceboard constructions that had been demoted from root cellar — was furnished with cruel, nightmare versions of that which in the civilised world are described as 'games'.

There was a darts board hanging on the far wall with a standard-distance toe-line but which, itself, was roughly one-tenth the size of a regulation board, and there were the standard three blue darts but only two red. Hard and wobbly stools stood around a backgammon table the dice of which had only ones on all sides. There was a quite nice, full-sized skittle alley, with normal pins and a shiny, flat surface, but the balls were yarn. The bagatelle table was mounted at a 45 degree angle.

"I understand that the idea is to…" Here, I believe, Ivor was quoting sarcastically, "…frustrate and recreate the catalytics which guests might encounter in their regular lives, in an environment in which their usual vices and coping mechanisms are denied them."

"Diabolical, isn't it?" Henny pistoned the cue ball at what I would later learn was the only one of a standard fifteen reds. She missed. "Rather puts one in mind of the haunted roulette wheel at Deauville, doesn't it Anty?" Henny provided context for Ivor, "It famously landed on zero eight times in a row — from when Anty sat down to when he retired to the bar."

"I thought you didn't know one another," said Ivor with Wittershimmy suspicion.

"Only as occasional and coincidental co-conspirators," Henny whimsied. "When did our ships first pass in the night, Anty? Was it when we were both swept up in that raid on the Fat Kat Klub or was it the jockeying scandal at Harringay?"

"Isn't Harringay a dog-coursing track?" asked Ivor.

"Hence the scandal." Henny nodded in stern recollection but then snapped her fingers. "I know — it was the Ample Merriweather Memorial Scavenger Hunt."

"Which year?" I took a seat at the cards table, as one does, and shuffled the deck. "I didn't compete this year, in light of my official observer capacity, with specific authority over the llama inventory."

"'28, I think. I say, Anty, whatever happened to Ample Merriweather?"

"Well, let's see…" As I shuffled the deck, I noted that there were no face cards and a surplus of twos. "He once got his thumb stuck in a magnum of champagne which he couldn't just break because it was full. He stayed like a full day until Carnedy suggested shaking the bottle. Popped right out."

"No, I mean to say, how did he die?"

"Ample Merriweather is dead?"

"Isn't he?"

"I don't think so," Instinctively, I dealt out respective hands of Twenty-one. I gave Henny two twos and myself one two and a dealer's card face down. "I saw him only yesterday at the club. Had his ring finger stuck in a bottle of Glen Glennegie."

"Then why is it called the Ample Meriweather Memorial Scavenger Hunt if Ample Meriweather isn't dead?" Henny tapped for another card.

"He very nearly did die during the first scavenger hunt," I dealt Henny the two of clubs. "Tried to pinch a pair of cami-knickers off a clothesline in Bermondsey."

"Ah. One more card, I think."

I dealt her another two of clubs. "Yes, the poor pickle. Might have got away if he hadn't got his foot stuck in a drain pipe."

Henny looked at her hand of three twos. "I should have split at four." She tapped for another card, which came up the two of hearts. "At any rate, I feel quite sure it was the '28 contest when we first met properly, if being manacled to the same duke can be considered meeting properly."

"You were manacled to Lord Chifney?" I gave Henny her third two of clubs. "Are you quite sure?"

"No, in fact, to be completely accurate, I was manacled to Sinjin Lord Ashby, and he was manacled to Lord Chifney. One more card, I think."

"Yes, that would explain it," I dealt Henny a two of laurel leaves. "It was a strong effort but ultimately doomed — turned out the third item on the scavenger list was 'two ducks'. Nevertheless, it was a lovely evening and weekend in the Bow Street nick except, like the Deauville phenomenon, it found its way into the society pages, and from there to the ken and condemnation of all the people who are my mother."

"That might have been my fault — I met a stringer for *Sighs and Whispers* at Barribault's, and he bet me a pint that I didn't have a front-page story for him." Henny leaned to confide in Ivor.

"He might have played my weakness, Inspector — I don't care what it is, I'll bet on it. Win or lose, pennies or pounds, horses or hounds, if there are odds I'll take them. My proudest moment is giving a newsagent on Fleet Street eighteen-to-one against that the next customer to buy a copy of *The Times* would be wearing a bowler."

"I see." Ivor regarded Henny in much the way he looks at me when I get to about the third act of an anecdote.

"Imagine the state of me when, not a minute later, the Bank of England let out for lunch and Fleet Street was a sea of bowlers but then, saved at the tape, Elizabeth Ponsonby walks up in a straw boater and a bow tie and buys every copy of *The Times* to give to friends because, if you can credit it, that very edition had a picture of her attending an American party in a straw boater and a bow tie."

Ivor blinked at me. There was something inexpressible in his gaze.

"Is this what brings you to Eden Bliss Paradise," I dealt her the fourth two of carriage wheels, "a predilection for gambling?"

"I regard it as a disease." She nodded solemnly at her cards. "And a cracking good time."

"And Doctor Smick was helping you break the habit, was he?" I asked.

"He did his best, the poor lamb. It's a nice rest, though." Henny smiled and cocked her head. "My favourite bit is probably the Unladening. I had a standing bet with your uncle that he'd snap before Colonel Brimble."

"I take it he's in the red," I guessed.

"Is he ever. I had to start giving him odds. He's a sportsman though, is your Uncle Pim. Bit of a sore loser."

"Can you describe for the benefit of Mister Boisjoly the events that led to the Doctor's retreat to his sanctuary?" officiated Ivor.

"It's as I told you — card, please… I'll stand." Henny stopped at her ninth two in a row. "Poor Pim lost another standing bet. He was doing so well. Doctor Smick was pestling on at the underlying cause of his anger and Pim just sat there, quietly simmering and then he proposed, if the Doctor liked and if he wouldn't mind just sitting still for a moment, Pim would be happy to twist his head off for him."

"And everyone dispersed to the compound to watch Doctor Smick climb his tree, did they?" I asked.

"There's very little passes for spectacle here, Anty," said Henny. "And I was hoping to make book on whether or not Diogenes would find the hawthorn berry I dropped into the doctor's trouser cuff when we were on our enforced nature walk in the woods."

I turned up the dealer card. It was one of the two tens in the deck.

"Just a second, Anty." Henny put her hand on mine. "What's the stake?"

"Pride of victory?"

"It's got to be for something," insisted Henny. "How much have you got on you?"

"I have this lovely tin flask." I withdrew from my breast pocket the empty ankle flagon. Henny stared as though I'd just casually produced the Hope Diamond.

"You got a flask past Diogenes?" she spoke in empty-church tones, but then composed herself and said, "Right. I anty a thousand pounds. In fact, never mind the game — I'll give you a thousand pounds for that flask. You'll take a cheque, I assume."

"I thought your weakness was gambling," I reminded her.

"Gambling, Anty, is a pastime," she said with cool distinction. "Whisky is a creed. Gimme."

"It's empty."

"How dare you, Boisjoly, toy with the affections of a girl?" Henny petitioned the inspector, "Isn't there a law of some sort?"

Ivor looked at her — and had been looking at her for some time — with that same dial of flat impatience that he's rested on me so very many times in the past. He said nothing. He just put his jotter into his pocket and then, as he'd done a thousand times already that day, reflexively took out his pipe. Henny yipped like someone had stepped on her tail while she was sleeping by the fire.

"You have tobacco?" Her voice cracked three octaves on 'acc'. "Spare a pinch to save a life, Inspector. When we're back in London I'll buy you something nice. A house. Would you like a house?"

"The inspector's pipe and pouch are empty, too. Diogenes got the lot," I said. "So, gambling, drinking, and smoking?"

"It's not enough?"

"Of course," I assured her. "One must find time for leisure, too."

"Miss Hackenit, are you aware of the existence of personal files that Doctor Smick apparently maintained on all his guests?" asked Ivor.

"Of course. I mean to say, I've never seen them, but it stands to reason he wrote it down somewhere. How would he even remember it all?"

"Do you recall any of it, Miss Hackenit?" Ivor put away, temporarily, his pipe, and retrieved his jotter.

"Not a word."

"Not even what was in your file?" doubted Ivor.

"You can't expect me to repeat any of that in front of the police, do you?" scoffed Henny. "Would you read a girl's diary?"

"In the execution of a murder investigation, yes, I would," said Ivor. "Are you saying that Doctor Smick had evidence of illegal activities?"

"Well, I mean, who's to say?" wondered Henny. "It's all relative, isn't it, illegal?"

"No."

"No, I suppose it isn't," acknowledged Henny. "I'm afraid I can't be certain, then, Inspector. I keep a very demanding schedule. If something slightly illegal slips in I can hardly be held responsible."

"Yes, you can, Miss Hackenit." Ivor put away his jotter and took out his pipe and clenched it menacingly. "Indeed, depending on the severity of these acts, they would constitute motive for murder."

CHAPTER EIGHT

The Juniper Journal of the Indolent Colonel

"I hope that you were keeping careful note, Inspector. I lost track of the vices which bring Miss Hackenit to Eden Bliss Paradise."

"All of them, apparently."

From within his rain barrel, his sagging snout resting on paws the size of hooves, Diogenes watched Ivor and me with rainy-day eyes as we crossed the muddy compound.

"Colonel Julius Brimble." Ivor referred to his jotter. "I take it you don't know this one, either?"

"Not very well," I confessed. "From the Suffolk Brimbles. Second son of Earl Oscar Brimble of Kettleby and, as such, was at a young age faced with a choice of a career in the military or a life of gadding and ladding about London."

"Hence the rank of colonel," supposed Ivor.

"One can hardly blame him," I sympathised. "It takes a chap of rare character and constitution to commit to the measure and pace. It's for life, you know, Inspector."

"He chose the easy path of achievement in the military, did he?"

"In a very real sense he did, yes," I said. "It was tradition at the time, as you're no doubt aware, that the second sons of earls should enter the army at no lower stamp than that of major. After eighteen brief terms at Oxford securing a third class degree in, I believe, mediaeval agriculture, Colonel Brimble quickly ascended the ranks, rising from major to colonel in one single, heady stride of thirty-two years."

"I thought you didn't know the man."

"I don't," I said. "Not by sight, at any rate, but his lore and legend are widely repeated in the quality clubs of London. The Juniper has a rotating role of Master of the Brimble Accounts. The position is largely ceremonial, because keeping track of the colonel is mainly a matter of checking in with Bow Street Magistrates' Court, and it's a rare day when there's not a Juniper on the docket. I myself appeared twice this month."

"You appeared before the courts twice in one month?" mazed Ivor.

"I did," I confessed. "I forgot about the other three summonses till just now."

"And Colonel Brimble manifests a similar respect for the law of the land, does he?" Ivor halted the advance at the bank of the marshy pond or pondy marsh.

"And yet he's never enjoyed the hospitality of the nick," I revealed. "Poor chap's unacquainted with the universal standard for savoury, as set by slow-fried bacon taken at Claridge's breakfast buffet the morning of release after a week at Bow Street lockup."

"All thanks, I assume, to connected friends."

"Let us stop at connected," I suggested. "It's widely understood that relations between the colonel and his wife's brother, Bow Street magistrate Sir Eustace Brittle, are coldly cordial. Where is he now?"

"Behind that copse of trees, when last seen." Ivor pointed with his pipe, which had once again popped into his hand, at a point where the bank of the pond curved out of sight around the treeline. "So the judge let Brimble off with a fine, did he?"

"Not even that. Whenever Colonel Brimble has come up before Sir Eustace, acting no doubt on the advice of the colonel's wife, in lieu of a custodial prison term or exemplary fine he has committed him to a course of treatment at Eden Bliss Paradise Health Resort."

"This place is his sentence?"

"Based on evidence gathered to date, Inspector, I'd prefer a week in the nick," I said. "Wouldn't you?"

"I daresay I would, yes." Ivor illustrated the point by stepping in a sinkhole and dropping his pipe into the mud. "Oh, pox." He recovered the pipe and a pound and a half of Epping Forest. "Hang on — 'whenever' he's come before the magistrates? How many times has Brimble been sentenced to a term of drying out?"

"Seven."

"Seven!"

"Well, eight, technically, but terms three and four were served concurrently," I accounted. "They had tickets for Wimbledon."

"I take it, then, the colonel's vice is drink."

"Only in the sense that he's hopelessly addicted to the stuff," I said. "His real problem is initiative."

"Lacks motivation, does he?" Ivor knocked his pipe against a tree, dislodging a purely symbolic quantity of mud. "Not an atypical problem for drinkers, in my experience."

"No, his problem isn't inertia, as such, it's electric impulse," I explained. "It's so that his default, undiluted state is indolent, but get a few drinks into him — a task as easily done as said — and he becomes a whir of misdirected industriousness. A few drinks later and he's more slothful than ever but by then, typically, the police have taken a hand."

"And he ends up here."

"He ends up here," I confirmed. "Most recently, after a casual soak at a seeing-off do for an old soldier who'd managed to fade away, the colonel came to the realisation — these sombre occasions are often conducive to moments of self-discovery — that he'd never before piloted a barge."

"And so…"

"And so he set about straight away to remedy the oversight, and found a canal boat moored at Limehouse Cut, looking for all the world to the colonel, in an advanced state of lubricated mourning, like community property. It even came ready equipped with a tow-mule and after only an hour or so fiddling with some complicated knots Colonel Brimble and Cloppy — the mule's name, it came to be later read into the court record, was Cloppy — set out. Things were going swimmingly, doubtless in the main because there's little to do when your barge is being towed by a mule who knows the way, and so Colonel Brimble, suffering from ennui after so quickly mastering helmsmanship, roamed the vessel and discovered that he'd accidentally commandeered a hold-load of whisky."

"Accidentally," repeated Ivor.

"Sir Eustace took exception to this characterisation of events as well," I noted. "However it was, Colonel Brimble soon cured himself of his burst of initiative, and Cloppy took the colonel and the barge all the way to Three Mill Island where he traded the remaining whisky for three sacks of oats."

"For a barge load of whisky?"

"Cloppy was an experienced navigator," I said. "But a poor negotiator."

The spongy bank curved into the tree line and onto a trapped puddle of a lagoon, quiet and confined and enclosed by pines. A small pier formed of rough planks and softwood pilings gently rotted at the top of the bay, and tied to it was a wooden skiff. In the little rowboat was a happily hunched figure in full evening dress, idly monitoring a spot in the water marked by the point where it met his fishing line. There was nothing military about the man's bearing at all, indeed, he presented a notably civilian absence of discipline about his dress, shaving habits, and weeks since he'd last combed his hair. He had thick white whiskers in the style of the military, which had gone to seed in the style of an English garden. The tuxedo was no contrast to any of this, and in fact it looked like a suit that had always dreamed of the simple life. I had a tweed three-piece like that once. Vickers gave it to the chap who does our chimneys, after which they both — the suit and Vickers, I mean to say — seemed much happier.

"Good afternoon, Colonel," Ivor ahoyed from the bank. Colonel Brimble raised his head and searched the waters in his immediate field of vision before giving a sigh and turning towards us.

"Oh, hullo, Inspector. And Mister Boisjoly, I presume."

"Call me Anty, if you fancy," I invited. "You were forewarned?"

"Your uncle mentioned you'd be coming to rescue him." The colonel slowly returned his attention to his fishing. "Wish I had a nephew."

"Quite sure you don't, Colonel?" I asked. "I feel we're legion."

"None to rescue me from this chamber of horrors. I've just got… what's his name, Ralph or Edwin or some such… wouldn't pull me out the way of a speeding train unless and until we'd settled terms." The colonel shook his head slowly at the still water. "Look at what that doctor's got me doing."

"Fishing?"

"Rowing!" scorned the colonel. "He said the exercise would do me good." He then appeared to quote sarcastically. "'Exercise exorcises the spirits from the spirit.' Have you ever heard such twaddle?"

"I expect he meant the exercise attendant with actually rowing the boat," I suggested.

In slow surmise, the colonel's gaze followed the rope which tethered the little boat to the pier.

"Yes, I suppose he did, now you point it out."

"You know, Colonel…" I tested the strength of the pier and found it wobbly but scamp-worthy, "…the doctor is no longer in a position to enforce the prescription. His focus is now doubtless on matters more eternal."

"I know it," sighed the colonel. "And now I suppose there's going to be a lot of bother."

"I'm afraid that's rather unavoidable in the case of cessation by sedation," I said. "Happily, though, we're in the hands of none other than Inspector Ivor Wittersham of the Yard, whose breezy banter and easy manner light the way from the galleries of the Old Bailey to the gallows of Pentonville, even when denied tobacco. Nevertheless, the point I'm making is that the doctor's orders can be considered, taking a liberal view, suspended."

The colonel scanned the treeline like an army scout.

"Yes. I'd have thought that, too. That… that novitiate, always going on about nature and health and all that ripe tripe…"

"Nurse Dalimore," I dispensed.

"Dalimore. That's it." Brimble started and his fishing line split the water. "She tells me nothing's changed, and I have to see out my treatment, as arranged, or she'll inform on me, as arranged."

"She'll tell the courts, will she?"

"She'll tell my wife," simmered the colonel, as one recounting foul menaces sworn by pirates on a starless midnight. "She's a lovely woman, the missus. I won't hear a word against her." The colonel raised his fishing rod in a 'make no mistake' gesture. "But she can often be a razor-tongued harpy tyrant." He lowered the rod gently, such as not to disturb the fish. "Sweetest woman in the world, apart from that."

"And her brother is a judge," I pointed out, helpfully.

"Sir Eustace Brittle." The colonel said this as though he had strong doubts that this was, in fact, his real name. "Thinks he can exile me to the forest."

77

"Which, in fact, he can," I helped once again.

"Yes, I suppose he can," acknowledged the colonel as though the awful truth was only just then striking home. "You can see why a chap might be feeling a little persecuted, then."

"You feel the sentence to be disproportionate to the crime," interpreted Ivor.

"Perhaps on this one occasion, no. I accept that my actions with regards the barge and Cloppy the donkey may have warranted a symbolic response." The colonel mused on the still waters for a moment before adding, "After all, justice must not only be done, but must also seem to be done."

"Be seen," corrected Ivor with sharp edges. "Lord Hewart, Lord Chief Justice, said justice must also be *seen* to be done."

"Well, there you go then," countered the colonel. "Don't you think a token fine levied in a public court is a good deal more visible than banishment to the wilderness?"

"He has a point, Inspector."

"It's a conspiracy, you understand," explained the colonel.

"You believe dark forces are afoot, Colonel?" I asked.

"I do." Brimble once again scanned the treeline. "I'm normally a very cautious man, you understand. I tend to take refreshment at my club, where women aren't allowed, or Belle Arome, which has a strict policy against non-smoking, or the bar car of The Flying Scotsman — the wife thinks I golf."

"Not really."

"No, not really," acknowledged the colonel. "She thinks I watch golf."

"Extraordinary that there remain those who claim you lack initiative," I said.

"Well, just so," agreed Brimble. "My wife and her brother, to take two examples to hand. And it was Mrs Brimble's attempt to address that reputation that got me sent up last time — It was she who volunteered me for that auction."

"Ah, yes," I recalled. "The Affair of the Tadcaster Hammer."

"You know the circumstances."

"I do."

"Then you know that I'm entirely blameless."

"Ehm…"

"It's Mrs Brimble — sweetest woman who ever drew breath, you understand, and anyone claiming I said different is inviting an action for libel — it's my wife who, without consulting me, put my name up for auctioneer of the Tadcaster charity rubbish market for foundling nobility."

Ivor's eyebrows regarded mine and said, 'Is this worth a listen?' and my eyebrows replied that yes, it most certainly was.

"I have no talent for auctioneering," admitted the colonel with admirable candour. "And I certainly had no inclination to dedicate an entire Thursday tea time to Lady Tadcaster's benevolent affair in aid of Lady Tadcaster's ego."

"Surely not," I encouraged. "You weren't expected to sacrifice an entire tea."

"Longer, if anything," miffed the colonel. "It was meant to start just after lunch, and I'm the sort of chap that needs inspiration before he really gets going."

"Whatever did you do?" I wondered, theatrically.

"I could hardly let the wife down," recalled Brimble loyally. "She'd have quite literally eviscerated me. Have you ever been an auctioneer?"

"I have," I said. "I'm the designated caller at my club each Epiphany when we sell off the umbrellas forgotten in the cloak room during the course of the year. The money we raise goes to buying surplus umbrellas."

"Then you know the experience can be quite trying to the nerves, and I find I respond well in the circumstance to a bit of whisky and plain water. I allowed myself a drop and took to the podium and, even if it's me saying so, I accounted for myself admirably."

"The auction was a success, was it?"

"Sold the lot," bragged the colonel. "Baroness Bellingham's paintings of hot-air balloons…"

"Self-portraits, I think you'll find."

"…Lord Snowsill-Willit's memoirs…"

"Purchased by Lady Snowsill-Willit," I provided, "with the specific objective of burning them."

"…Lady Selwyn-Bluntly's home-made jams…"

"Acquired by the War Office, for research purposes."

"…Lady Tadcaster's silverware…"

"And there begins the legend," I said, mainly to the inspector. "Lady Tadcaster's silverware wasn't on the docket, was it, Colonel?"

"Not in any official manner, no," he admitted. "I assumed, at the time, that it was an oversight."

"Nor was Sir Clancy Tadcaster's collection of Reubens…"

"Not as such."

"…nor his Rolls Royce Phantom."

"Instructions were unclear," claimed the colonel. "And when operating on a drop of whisky I tend to take the broad view."

"And for that you were condemned to a custodial period in Epping Forest," I said in closing.

"Not exclusively that, no." The colonel raised his line out of the water and we could see that there was no bait nor, for that matter, a hook. "I sold Sir Clancy's wine cellar."

"Yes, you did, didn't you, Colonel," I recounted for Ivor's benefit. "You sold it for a pound, if the Juniper Brimble Accounts are a reliable source. And to whom did you sell it, Colonel?"

"Myself."

"Possibly not entirely in keeping with the spirit of the occasion," judged Ivor, "but within the law. I would at least have thought you'd have had a solid defence in the absence of clear terms."

"I would have done, yes," agreed the colonel, "but appearing in court can be quite trying to the nerves, and I find I respond well in the circumstance to a bit of whisky and plain water…"

"Did the court not lose patience with this course of treatment?" wondered Ivor. "I understand that you've been ordered to Eden Bliss Paradise some seven times."

"Eight," corrected the colonel. "It's odd you should say that. In fact, it never occurred to me that anything like what might be called results were expected. I just assumed Mrs Brimble and Sir Eustace wanted me to keep a low profile for a few weeks, but it turns out they were surprised at my frequent acts of recidivism. Apparently my wife was of the opinion that Doctor Smick was showing me some form of favouritism." He spun 'favouritism' as though it was a punchline, and gestured about us, making reference to the general all, to emphasise the point. "So she accompanied me up here this time, and met the doctor and had a tour of the place. She was already persuaded, though, from the moment that dog made her surrender the medicinal absinthe she keeps in a vial in her walking stick. After that she knew that this place was a stygian island of misery and despair, and so she was quite content leaving me here."

"And how long ago was that, Colonel?" I asked.

"It's very difficult to say." The colonel gazed around at the forest as though evaluating a change in season. "The routine is very intense — it's patterned closely on the course of penal labour laid down for violent offenders. Between treatments and tasks, working the treadmill and oakum picking…"

"Doctor Smick had you picking oakum?" marvelled Ivor.

"Near as." The colonel searched the immediate area and, spotting his oars on the pier, issued them a resentful sneer. "He's got me doing all this rowing. It's interminable, and if you've ever served time you'd know that pointless labour causes one day to blur into the next."

"Oh, I know it does," I assured him. "I myself, only last month, was sentenced to issue a personal apology to every single shopkeeper in the Burlington Arcade. Took them all to the Criterion bar and that's the last thing I remember until the following Sunday."

"That's the true, quiet, exquisite evil of this place." The colonel slowly reeled in his line. "I could just about manage the backbreaking drudgery and browbeating but…" once again, Colonel Brimble surveyed the forest for spies, "…they don't allow any alcohol. I mean to say, none at all, there's not any wine with dinner, no port afterwards, no sherry for tea, no breakfast gin. I'm at the breaking point." .

Ivor referred to his jotter. "My understanding is that you arrived yesterday, Colonel."

"Did I?" Brimble shook his head in slow disbelief. "That explains it — I believe that I've forgotten what whisky tastes like."

"Still spiffing," I assured him.

He rose on what would have been impressively sure sea legs had it not become instantly apparent that the boat was aground in about six inches of still water. We handed him aboard the pier and he leaned in close.

"Anty, my dear boy. Have you anything at all? Even a drop would do a world of good."

"Diogenes got the lot, I'm afraid, Colonel."

"Is that the dog?"

"It is."

"Miserable creature."

"He's only doing his duty, Colonel," I said, coolly. "If it's any consolation at all, he doesn't appear to enjoy his work."

"If we could return to the events of earlier today, Colonel…" led Ivor.

"Again, Inspector?" wearied Brimble. "How many times must we go over it?"

"This would be the second time," Ivor reminded him. "And during the first instance you required a lie-down. Twice."

"Oh, very well." The colonel handed me his fishing rod. "Reel that in the rest of the way, will you Anty?" He trod carefully back to the bank. "Let us walk back to my lodgings. I feel quite fatigued after an outing on the water."

Ivor followed, opening his jotter. "You were present at this 'Unladening'?"

"I was." Brimble nodded with brooding lassitude. "We all were. It's a rule."

"And Doctor Smick didn't ingest anything during the meeting?" asked Ivor.

"No one did. Another rule. There are a lot of rules here."

"You described the atmosphere as 'caustic'," Ivor read from his notes.

"We had only met, Inspector," said the colonel. "I was unsure what sort of language you would tolerate."

"I mean to say, you don't recall any one of you to be any more irate with Doctor Smick than any other."

"Not very noticeably, no," recalled the colonel as he contemplated a worryingly slippery fallen log in his path. "Apart from Pimsloe, if you count him."

"Why wouldn't I count him?" wondered Ivor.

"Well, he was the only one of us to actually say, in those very words, that he was going to murder the doctor." The colonel executed a deft hop over the log. "I thought that made him exceptional. Admirable, even."

"And what was it that provoked my uncle?" I asked. "Typically he's self-possessed to a fault."

"I expect it was just Smick's usual brutal interrogation tactics," speculated Brimble. "Oh, and Pimsloe was quite irked that the doctor had taken away his odds book."

"Yes, Uncle Pim mentioned that..." I stopped briefly and watched Colonel Brimble step gingerly over a mud puddle the size of a saucer. "When did this occur, Colonel?"

"This morning." Brimble stood his ground on the banks of the puddle. "I mean to say, this is my understanding."

"And do you know how it is that Doctor Smick came to be aware of the existence of the odds book?" I asked.

Brimble traced the puddle with the toe of his shoe. "No, no idea. He just seems to know things, don't you know."

"This is what Uncle Pim said, too," I recalled. "But if Doctor Smick knew about the book, why did he only impound it this morning? My uncle's been here for two weeks, and has visited several times in the past, and I feel quite confident that he's never failed to make book on everything from mosquito bite accumulators to... something else which occurs in the wilderness — I fear I have exhausted my knowledge thereof. In any case, clearly there was something unusual about this morning's events, wasn't there, Colonel?"

"Well, as I say, one day is very much like the next in forced labour."

"You told the doctor about Uncle Pim's bookmaking operation," I barristered. "May I ask why?"

The colonel, in a clear demonstration of his level of ill-ease, traced a circle the other direction around the puddle.

"Well. It's against the rules, isn't it?"

"It is," I agreed. "So is selling yourself the contents of an entire wine cellar for a quid. Had it anything to do, Colonel, with Doctor Smick's secret files?"

Colonel Brimble invested more energy in his response than he'd probably put into his entire military career. His eyebrows took flight, he stepped back from the puddle with such alacrity that his arms waved in a reflexive emergency balancing operation, he huffed and coughed like a man answering serious charges in the House of Lords, and his complexion — already very close to transparent — took on a pallor so devoid of colour that it all but glowed.

"Secret files?" he eked. "Doctor Smick had secret files?"

CHAPTER NINE

The Tacit Asset of the Cynical Basset

Rain comes upon a dense wood in a very theatrical fashion. For one thing, like a scene change, it's announced. There's a looming shush as of, initially, a foretelling breeze, dashing from tree to tree, shaking them by their branches and warning them of dark times to come. Then the rain itself actually falls but it doesn't immediately penetrate the canopy of forest. It stops overhead and builds up volume and weight and then, in a stroke, the curtain rises and the deluge comes, as though from some celestial spigot.

Ivor and I dashed back to the compound — Colonel Brimble said he'd prefer to drown rather than run — and selected for shelter a low, leaky, leaning of logs and leaves. It appeared to be some sort of barracks or, possibly, a jury-rigged brig, relic of an era since man started to explore Epping Forest but before any major evolutions in penal reform.

I would have said the interior was about the size of that of a fishing lodge, had I ever been to a fishing lodge, and there were orderly camp beds and a makeshift brazier formed of damp soil and something which, when burned and put into contact with damp soil, smells like a hangover. The rain sloshed onto the roof in a sustained hum and dripped through countless holes in a jazzy, repeating rhythm.

"Let's get a fire lit." Ivor stood dripping in the doorway, looking at the curtain of rain. "Then I suppose I must take charge of Doctor Smick's files."

A neat pyramid of firewood was stacked next to the fire pit, directly beneath a steady stream of rainwater from a hole in the roof. If only to complete the picture, Ivor withdrew his box of soaking matches and looked at them with a sort of resigned dejection.

"No sense both of us getting soaked." Ivor handed over the soggy, sagging match box. "See what you can do with that."

I had dressed, as I do everything, optimistically, and was thusly sorely unprepared for the weather. Ivor was always — rain, shine, or lengthy periods indoors — prepared for a monsoon. It was the merest logic that he should be the one to go and secure Doctor Smick's files.

The inspector stepped into and was immediately consumed by the storm. I quickly dispensed with my one task in determining that there were no salvageable matches in the box and so occupied myself with abating the solitude of an earthen refuge in a remote spot of a dense forest in a denser storm. I swaddled myself in the sheets and blankets and huddled onto a cot and listened to the drone of the water cycle and, in due course, was hypnotised to sleep.

Minutes or hours may have passed but certainly the torrent still hissed and trilled when I awoke. However the darkness and cold and even the hovering damp had evanesced on the dry, homey heat of a crackling, snapping fire. A silhouette crouched over the conflagration, feeding it twigs and leaves and prodding it to greater things. The obscure giant seemed to notice me in the same instant that I noticed him and he unbent to his full, towering height. His flickering, conflicting shadows dashed in duplicates across the walls of the sanctuary as he withdrew from the fire a vessel of shimmering steel.

The shadow man turned to me and spoke in flat, final tones, "I have made tea, sir."

"Not a moment too soon, Vickers," I welcomed. "I hope you weren't put to much trouble returning to Eden Bliss Paradise."

"None to speak of, sir." Vickers established a rudimentary tea beachhead on a cylinder of firewood and poured me a tin mug of

Kensington parlour. "Which is to say, in fact, that I have no recollection of how I regained the compound."

"You don't remember returning through Epping Forest?" I marvelled. "Surely Mister Livesy brought you with his sulky and immense horse."

"That's precisely what eludes my recall, sir." Vickers distractedly helped himself to a mug of tea. "I certainly returned with the horse and carriage, but I wasn't accompanied by Mister Livesy."

"You didn't murder him, did you Vickers? Ivor will be most vexed. He's already stretched to a thread by tobacco withdrawal."

"I don't believe so, no…" Vickers nodded dubiously.

"Let us retrace your steps," I proposed, as the hot tea began its vital work on my faculties. "How did you find me here?"

"In fact that was pure chance. This was the first shelter I found after following the dog out of the woods."

"Ah, so Diogenes found you. Were you lost?"

"I think that goes without saying."

"At the risk of spoiling the surprise, Vickers, can I assume that if Diogenes found you that he also found the whisky?"

"I fear so, sir." Vickers stood at the doorway to the storm and sipped his tea philosophically. "I had to leave it all in the forest."

"Then where did we get tea?"

"The dog didn't appear to object to the tea, once I'd given up everything else."

"It's too late now, Vickers, and I don't mean this as a reproach, but should we find ourselves in similar circumstances, and it comes down to a choice between whisky and tea…"

"I don't believe that I was offered a choice in the matter," said Vickers. "Diogenes just stared at me with a surprisingly persuasive countenance until I divested myself of all food and drink."

"What do you suppose would have happened if you'd just walked on?" I wondered.

"I'm told by Mister Livesy that if Diogenes detects any forbidden substances at all, he will follow the subject until he surrenders the product or one of them dies."

"And how does Mister Livesy come to know this?" I asked.

"He provided the animal to the health resort, according to his account," explained Vickers. "Diogenes was not always as you see him now. Indeed, he was christened Chip."

"First born son, was he?"

"It was an abbreviation of Chipper," said Vickers, "on account of his energetic conviviality."

"Diogenes? Energetic conviviality? What happened to it?"

"Sadly, circumstances conspired to disabuse him of what had been, apparently, a naive and optimistic nature."

"One might even say Boisjolian."

"The very word, sir," agreed Vickers. "Mister Livesy maintains strong views regarding the utility of optimism as a quality of character, particularly that of dogs, horses, and…" A cloud of recollection passed over Vicker's face, "...those in domestic service."

"And what was it cured Diogenes of this crippling optimism?"

"No one thing, as I understand it," said Vickers. "He was rejected by his mother and, on that same day, separated from his siblings, all of whom were adopted by small children and taken to estates in the country. Diogenes, although he remained hopeful, was exchanged for services rendered to a gang of confidence tricksters, for whom he served as the key device in an artifice in which he was presented as a rare breed of Bavarian Doxie."

"So young to be turned to a life of crime."

"Precisely, sir," continued Vickers. "And, indeed, when he grew too large to convincingly pass as a Dachshund, Diogenes was returned to Mister Livesy who then placed him with a family in Chelsea."

"Chelsea's nice. It's no Kensington, but it's not Hammersmith, either."

"The family in Chelsea returned Diogenes after three days," recounted Vickers, "when they realised that he clashed with the ground floor colour scheme."

"It's never an easy thing, matching a tawny and tan basset with the drapes."

"He was then adopted by a close confidant of Oswald Mosley, who sent him back because he could not be trained to reliably bark at poor people." Vickers grimaced into a painful past. "This was followed by a short apprenticeship as a ratter, where he contracted ringworm, canine distemper, and a fear of close spaces. He was then taken on as a tracking hound by a consulting detective who turned out to be a jewel thief, a companion dog for a home for orphan boys eventually exposed as a school for pickpockets, and as a member of a border patrol team, the other members of which ostracised him for his short stature and long ears."

"Oof," I sympathised. "Rather a lengthy list of woe for such a young dog. What is Diogenes, Vickers? Five?"

"Two," said Vickers. "The list goes on, I fear, and each time he was returned, Mister Livesy was gratified to observe that his enthusiastic conviviality was, by steps and measures, visibly reduced, until he was as you see him now, manifesting a character composed of what I would describe as penetrating distrust."

"Well spoken," I agreed. "When he settled that judgemental eye on Ivor and me as we crossed the compound earlier this evening I had nothing left to surrender, so I instead confessed to voting twice for my own entry in the Juniper spats design contest."

"Have we an entry in the Juniper spats design contest?"

"We do not," I said. "Hence the genius of my stratagem — it was to add verisimilitude when Spins Purley won with his chequerboard motif, for which I voted three times."

Vickers phlegmatic features took on a curious, concentrated countenance that I'd seen many times, and it typically precedes a revelation, the veracity of which is largely random but the entertainment value of which is consistently five stars with an encore.

"Something coming back to you, Vickers?" I prompted.

"Spats, sir…" Vickers regarded a leak in the ceiling. "I was fetching spats, in the jungle."

"A literal jungle, Vickers?" I queried. "Or do you refer to the metaphorical savage wilderness that is the spat and gaiter markets of central London?"

"It was in Burma, I believe, when I was acting as batman for your grandfather when he was offered the governorship of Thayetmyo."

"My grandfather, a Boisjoly, during a time of delicate and fragile negotiations at the epicentre of the arrayed military might of three empires, was offered a governorship of a vital and volatile trading port?"

"He had been lead bowler for the Earl of Northbrook's Calcutta county cricket side," explained Vickers.

"Ah, well then," I said. "Nevertheless, I don't recall what would doubtless have been the inimitable Boisjoly hand in destroying British influence in the entirety of mainland Southeast Asia had he accepted such a role."

"Your grandfather had a similar premonition, sir," agreed Vickers. "We set out immediately for Rangoon, where Mister Boisjoly Senior had a standing invitation from the East India Company to assume a role created specifically for him. Formally, he would preside over hospitality, but his duties consisted principally of embarrassing local dignitaries."

"I recall this, now," I recalled, now. "He was, let me think…"

"Boisjoly-in-residence."

"That was it," I concurred. "Well, that explains everything but the spats. And everything else."

"I'm sorry, sir. I was endeavouring to approach the matter systematically… more tea?"

"Have we more tea?"

"Ample, sir."

"Then yes. And then proceed."

Vickers distributed the cockle-warmer and then resumed his attitude of baffled concentration.

"We were a small party of some seven or eight household servants, two hussars, a croupier, a chef, and an interpreter who also served as occasional sommelier."

"Skeleton staff, for a proper ministry of dignitary embarrassing, I'd have thought."

"Your grandfather intended to train up some promising locals," explained Vickers. "But this was the entourage with which we made our way to Rangoon, following the Irrawaddy River as far south as Yaykyaw, after which we made our way through the jungle. About five miles inland your grandfather realised that he'd left behind several important items, such as his surrender uniform, his loaded dice, and, notably, his spats case."

"Were these not your responsibility?"

"I was merely his batman, at the time, sir," Vickers reminded me coolly. "Yaza was the spats boy, and he also functioned as master of games, in light of severe staffing shortages."

"Then why wasn't it he who had to go back for the spats?"

"Yaza was also left behind, as it happens. We departed quite hurriedly, in light of the pending appointment."

"Very like grandpapa," I reminisced. "Never one to let the grass grow in the face of the menace of duty."

"Aptly expressed, sir, yes," agreed Vickers. "However it was, it was I who was conscripted to make the return journey while the travel party sheltered with a regional sultan."

"And you got lost," I deduced.

"I did."

"And furthermore, the strain and circumstances were such that, after you became lost in Epping Forest, you found yourself back in the jungles of Burma."

"The conditions were uncannily similar," contended Vickers. "On both occasions I relied on the homing instinct of a horse, and there was a monsoon."

"The Burmese horse didn't know his way home?"

"He did, in fact, but his home was not Thayetmyo. We were soon lost in woven jungle and I was forced to survive on roots and berries."

"You had no supplies?"

"Only a substantial reserve of vermouth and caviar."

"Oh." I lowered my tea respectfully. "Dire, Vickers."

"Yes, sir. Each on its own is a powerful appetite stimulant. Taken together, as you know, they produce an effect of cavernous hunger."

"Like waking up in a cell on a Sunday morning after stealing a policeman's helmet on a Friday night."

"Precisely the analogy I was going to draw." Vickers nodded grave accord.

"And when all you have to eat is that which enhances the appetite even more..."

"I soon found myself foraging for roots and berries," concurred Vickers, "but roots and berries, even when they can be found, are scarcely comparable to caviar and vermouth."

"So you returned to the source and fed the famine."

"Deftly put, sir."

"Like Erysichthon of Thessaly," I said. "The more he ate, the hungrier he became."

"The parallel had not escaped me, sir, even and perhaps especially at the time." Vickers gazed metaphorically into the flames. "The experience also put me in mind of the torments of Tantalus."

"Or Barley Babbacombe," I said, perhaps, stretching the point. "Once spent an afternoon and the rest of his operating capital for the month at Barribault's, draining the place of its entire supply of Beluga caviar and vodka-and-vermouth martinis. And then, as suddenly as flicking a switch, he dashed across the street to The Hound and Huntsman where he traded his father's watch for an entire steak and kidney pie and a plate of chips."

"I can fully sympathise with Mister Babbacombe," Vickers commiserated. "The memory, if it needs be said, has endured, and so when I found myself in similar circumstances — in the woods in the rain with a horse, subsisting on roots and berries, the years fell away, and I found myself in the jungles of Burma…"

"Just two tickers, Vickers," I dickered. "Why were you eating roots and berries? Was the entire purpose of the exercise not to smuggle Alladin's lunch counter back with you?"

Vickers cocked his head like a spaniel on the verge of an epiphany, and then spoke with the rote of one retrieving an incantation from the fog of a distant youth, *"Terrine de porc,* hard-boiled quail eggs, Iberian cured ham, onion and lime chutney, two lamb shoulders, four roast pheasants, a dozen Mowbray pies, a dozen Balmoral scones, clotted cream, a case of Bollinger, and a case of *Chateau Roque, Ballan Miré Merlot* — the '24, which I judged would travel better than the '23."

"All that slipped your mind, did it?"

"Regrettably so," regretted Vickers with sad sincerity. "I was entirely preoccupied with the object of the journey."

"My grandfather's spats."

"Yes, sir."

"And where is all this treasure now?"

The faithful gentleman's personal gentleman gazed sadly and meaningfully out at the storm.

"I can only say for certain that it's somewhere deep in the woods."

"Diogenes was able to find you, in this weather, deep in the woods?" I gogged. "What an extraordinarily gifted snout that animal has."

"I may have been thrashing about somewhat, in fact, with a branch," said Vickers as though confessing something which, it turned out, he was. "I thought there was a tiger."

"A tiger."

"It turned out to be a forest hare."

"A rabbit?"

"It was an abnormally large specimen."

"Good job Diogenes was there to chase the monster off," I cheered. "Have we retraced far enough to work out what became of Mister Livesy?"

"Oh dear."

"Oh good," I surmised. "It's come back to you."

"I fear that I may have locked Mister Livesy in a feed shed."

"Well, at least he'll have plenty to eat, assuming he eats oats," I said. "Do you know if Mister Livesy eats oats, Vickers?"

"Uncannily, sir, I do." Vickers spoke with the tone of a man shaking off the effects of a champagne bottle to the back of the head. "It's all he eats. Mister Livesy is persuaded to the point of evangelistic of the health benefits of porridge, and indeed it was just this conviction that compelled me to resort to extreme measures."

"Wouldn't see the light with regards to hard-boiled quail eggs, I take it."

"Precisely, sir," confirmed Vickers. "I offered him as much as ten pounds. I would have gone higher, but it was clear that his were deeply ingrained principles, and ten pounds was all I had in ready capital."

"You did the right thing, Vickers. Men who eat only oatmeal are not to be trusted," I advised him. "They're like parsons who drink only tea or schoolboys who've never read Scott — the best you can hope for is the inevitable and spectacular public paroxysm of regret which, while entertaining, is all but impossible to plan for. How did you manage to lock Mister Livesy in a feed barn?"

"When it became clear that he wasn't going to agree to allow me to transport the contraband to Eden Bliss Paradise, I allowed him to believe that he had convinced me to bring instead ten pounds worth of oatmeal," recalled Vickers. "That is a very substantial amount of oatmeal. While he was shovelling it into bags, I put the handle of a pitchfork through the latch, loaded up the sulky, and drove into the woods."

"How did you mean to find your way here?"

"I believe that I thought that I would recall the route, sir," said Vickers, searchingly. "I didn't."

Further regrets, sadly, were left unexplored when Ivor crashed in out of the rain, as through a stained glass window. There is no more water-tight detective inspector in all of Britain, and once he'd unsealed himself from his hermetic trench coat, spatterdashes, and gaiters, and uncorked the lined fedora, he might have just returned from a dusty attic, where he'd been eating dry cream crackers.

"Mister Vickers," welcomed Ivor. Then he lowered his voice. "Did you bring tobacco?"

"He didn't," I reported. "But the good news is, he didn't bring any oatmeal, either."

"Tobacco…" mused Vickers, as on some youthful fancy.

"Yes, Mister Vickers…" urged Ivor. "Did you manage to secure some?"

"Yes, sir. A tin of Dunhill…"

"That will do nicely."

"…which I abandoned somewhere in the woods."

Ivor didn't reply, except with a sad study of the pipe which he held in both hands, like a little boy with a broken toy.

"However, the subject of tobacco puts me in mind of something else," recalled Vickers, "Most of the provisions are lost in the forest, but I was able to withhold and conceal a bottle of Glen Glennegie."

"However did you get it past Diogenes?" I wanted to know.

"I don't know…" Vickers spoke with a disengaged tone as he, seemingly unconsciously, poured the inspector a cup of tea. "…I'm not certain that I did — I buried it at the base of a tree."

"Excellent, Vickers — now we just have to find a tree in Epping Forest."

"I mean to say, a particular tree, sir," said Vickers. "Notable because there were several cigarette ends at its base."

"Oh ho," I observed. "That's a most particular tree indeed, for a health resort. My overcoat, if you please, Vickers."

"You're not going out in this," doubted, for some reason, Ivor.

"Perhaps you misheard, Inspector, but there's a bottle of Glen Glennegie out there in, as you so aptly termed it, 'this'. It's alone and, probably, frightened. It's a very delicate distillation. Is it the four-year '26, Vickers?"

"Yes, sir."

"There you go. Young and naive and, happily, complemented to a nicety with just a drop of rainwater."

"We have a more pressing matter," claimed Ivor.

"I dispute that."

"Doctor Smick's files…" countered Ivor.

"Oh, right," I dithered. "What do they say?"

"I don't know," said Ivor. "They've been stolen."

CHAPTER TEN

The Misleading Mystery of the Missing Missives

"I thought you had the only key to the doctor's filing cabinet," I said.

"This is what Nurse Dalimore claimed, at least," agreed Ivor. "And, indeed, it appears the doctor was the last person to open it."

"How could you possibly know that?"

"Come along and I'll show you."

Vickers remained to tend the fire and, doubtless, to pass a few nostalgic moments in Burma, and Ivor and I went out once again into the elements.

"Why don't you have a proper raincoat?" wondered Ivor as we sloshed through the compound.

"I lack your strength of character, Inspector," I admitted. "I dislike being laughed at."

"Well, look at you now."

"Good point, well made," I conceded. "However under normal circumstances, in London I mean to say, I'm able to employ an artifice that my mother taught me when I was but a lad — you might want to take note of this — she advised me to come in out of the rain. In the spirit of full disclosure, what she actually said was that she doubted I had the sense to do so, but the lesson stuck."

Doctor Smick's forest abode was at the top of the compound between the dining hall/games room on the one side and the Smoking Lounge and Serenity Salon on the other, and it had the design and dimensions of the cottage of a clean-living gnome. It was formed of a stone foundation and floor, wattle and daub walls, and a roof of sloppy and smelly thatch, dark and heavy with wet. It did, however, have a little tin chimney from which puffed a friendly call to the hearth.

"What ho, Babbs," I greeted a grim-faced Babbage, who was sitting on a log before a flickering fire in a pot-bellied stove, abusing it with a stick.

"I've looked everywhere…" announced the coroner, "…there's not a strand of tobacco."

He had looked. There was little furniture in the spartan cell but what drawers and boxes and cases there were had been thoroughly turned out and gone through. All that remained closed was a tin lockbox on a small writing desk, the left back leg of which had been replaced with a broom handle. There was not another scrap of paper in the room.

"You found it locked," I divined, "but with all the contents removed."

"Almost all." Ivor unlocked the box, which opened as a metal drawer. In it was a well-thumbed blotter. "Your uncle's odds book."

"And if he took the book away from my uncle only this morning, then Smick has obviously opened the box since then," I calculated. "Meaning that even if that's not the only key, no one could have taken the files without the doctor's knowledge."

"So Smick himself must have removed and, presumably, destroyed the files," concluded Ivor.

We all looked at the little pot-bellied fire.

"I made this fire," announced Babbage, as though he feared we might claim it, "and the stove was cold when I did."

"Then what could he have done with them?" wondered Ivor. "You've thoroughly searched the place, you say, Mister Babbage."

"Satisfy my curiosity, will you Inspector?" primed Babbage. "What interpretation did you put on it when I first said that I thoroughly searched the place? Did you think that I meant some other place? Or do the words 'search' or 'thoroughly' take on different meanings for you, depending on your mood?"

"We must be approaching dinner time, Inspector," I noted. "I propose that we join the others and bring that box with us, and observe the reactions of the guests. Whoever recognises the box will doubtless be the one who has the files."

The dining hall of Eden Bliss Paradise Health Resort was entirely in keeping with expectations, although there was a soupçon of London nostalgia in the windowless, adobe oubliette of an underpass that put me in mind of an urban underbelly that Dickens might have invented when in the mood to throw a proper crank at the class system.

In the middle of this room with the shape, glimmer, and charm of Islington Tunnel was, depending on one's definition of the word 'table', either one, long table, or several tables, two planks balanced on barrels, a bureau desk, and some crates in parade formation. To complete the Victorian Dickensian workhouse disposition of the room, or just because that was the most convenient place for it, at the head of the table was an iron cauldron of simmering oatmeal porridge.

"Do you like boiled horse feed, Inspector?" I asked, as we stood at the door breathing in the heady scene.

"Can it be smoked?"

"Not without a fight," I speculated. "It's hardy stuff. It can go in one end of a haggis and out the other practically unscathed."

The resident population of Eden Bliss Paradise ceased a sullen clamour and turned the collective attention on the metal box under Ivor's arm.

"The one who recognises it has the files, you say, Mister Boisjoly," mumbled Ivor.

"Extraordinary, isn't it?" I agreed. "They all must have the files."

A long journey by train and then by horse and carriage, a day spent in the mud and rain and cold, and the draws and drains of a murder investigation can conspire together to give a chap a ravenous appetite and, in the absence of unidentifiable bloated organic matter retrieved from the pond or a plate of boiled shoe leather, I gratefully accepted a bowl of unsweetened oatmeal porridge, dished out by Nurse Dalimore and delivered by Vickers.

"Not as offensive as expected," I said to Ivor. "Tastes a bit like warm snow, wouldn't you say?"

Apart from witty quips of that nature, including a cunning comparison of the storm to balmy Belgian beach weather, conversation was muted. I even had a second bowl or, at any rate, I had most of a second bowl before hitting in no uncertain manner that solid wall beyond which the next spoonful of unsweetened oatmeal porridge is as appetising as a mouthful of dry flour. By then the party was already dispersing and taking puddle-bark tea standing around the dining tumble or in the adjoining Games Room.

"I'll bet you I know what's in that box."

The first contestant was Uncle Pim, who cornered me by a damp patch on the wall between the dining and games rooms. He had changed for dinner from one set of flannel day wear to an almost indistinguishable suit of flannel evening wear, including a tiny tight bowtie and a corduroy waistcoat that was, like his daytime tweed waistcoat, missing a button. He glanced furtively about and toyed with the waistcoat button that he'd recovered from the pond and made the above-mentioned challenge.

"I feel quite sure that you can," I agreed.

"Be a sport, Anty," urged Pim in hushed tones, somehow effecting to hide behind his button. "I'll give you odds."

"Where would you write them down?"

"I thought as much." Pim glanced at the box on which rested Ivor's teacup. "I say, Anty, it's not as though it's evidence of any sort of crime…"

"Apart from illegal bookmaking."

"Well, exactly. Hardly a crime at all. You couldn't get it back for me…" Pim surveyed the field and took note that Ivor was in close conference with Nurse Dalimore before adding, "…discreetly."

"No, you're right, I couldn't," I agreed. "In fact, I couldn't get it back for you with a symphony performing Elgar. You knew your odds book was in the secret files box, then."

"Stands to reason," said Pim. "After Smick took it from me he went directly to his shack."

"Then what did he do?" I asked.

"Put it in his lockbox." Pim spoke as one describing the confiscation of an innocent set of conkers.

"I mean to say, what did he do after that?" I clarified.

"He came here."

"To the dining room?"

"The unladening room, at that time of day," reported Pim with weary irony.

"Would you have seen if he'd spoken to anyone along the way?"

"I certainly would have," my uncle assured me. "I accompanied him, trying to convince him to take the broadminded view."

"And everyone was here when you arrived?"

"Yes." Pim withdrew a handkerchief and polished his button in a manner calculated to express suspicion. "What are you on about, Anty? The book is with Smick's files, isn't it?"

"Your odds book is, indeed, in the lockbox."

"Well, listen, Anty, I don't need it back so much, although that would obviously be very welcome, but we neither of us want your mother to hear about it, do we?"

"Don't we?"

"You know what she'd do." Pim pointed the button at me menacingly. "She'd make you cut off my credit, and then... well, Anty, then I fear that I would have to cut off *your* track tips."

"Your last six certainties placed, respectively, sixth, sixth, eighth, ninth, not at all, and sixth."

"Well, there you go, Anty." Pim flipped the button, caught it mid-air, and slapped it down on his wrist. "I'm due a win." He checked the button. "Ha. Heads. Just as predicted."

"I see no reason why Mama should know about the odds book, Uncle Pimlico," I said. "I can't really speak to the rest of Smick's files on you, though."

"Rest?" Pim flipped his button but this time it escaped him. "What else is in there?"

"For the moment, Uncling, I cannot say. You don't know?"

"Not as such, no." Pim examined his button where it lay on the floor. "Pox — tails. It's about that absurd exaggeration at Chelmsford, isn't it?"

"What absurd exaggeration at Chelmsford?"

Pim retrieved his button and when he returned he was squinting sly suspicion.

"I mean to say..." I corrected for conditions, "...which absurd exaggeration at Chelmsford?"

"You haven't read that far in the files?"

"The lockbox presents many mysteries, Uncling. Why don't you just tell me about it?"

"I was robbed." Pim's voice lowered and his eyes widened with righteous umbrage.

"You were robbed at Chelmsford Racecourse?"

"In a very real sense, yes." Pim confirmed that the police presence remained a safe distance. "I had a tip straight from the paddock — Pickled Farthing in the third."

"Pickled Farthing failed to give satisfaction?"

"Spotted a patch of track at the second furlong that he liked, downed tools and settled in," reminisced Pim bitterly. "He'd be there to this day if I hadn't taken a hand."

"What sort of hand did you take?" I queried.

"You need to understand, Anty, I didn't go to Cheltenham to bet on Pickled Farthing," confided Pim. "I had it on very good authority that a severely underappreciated colt named Three White Socks with a starting price of nineteen-to-one was going to extend himself beyond all expectations."

"To which authority do you refer, Unk?" I asked. "You'll forgive me, but you have been known to put your faith in some spurious sources."

"That's as may be," dismissed Pim, "but not this time. You know Chivers?"

"Your valet, yes, I know Chivers."

"Well, the morning of the race — the very moment I'm studying the field in *Track and Turf,* mind you — Chivers comes in and lays out my socks."

"Chivers laid out three white socks?" I marvelled. "I confess, I might have received that as a sign from above myself."

"Well, no, in point of fact, he laid out a pair of brown argyles, but it was the very instant the odds on Three White Socks caught my eye," said Pim with a hushed awe. "And, if that's not enough which it clearly is, Chivers, in that very moment, said, 'your socks, sir.' I mean to say, Anty, what are the odds?"

"No, quite. Uncanny."

"Well, there you go." Uncle Pim resumed juggling his button with the air of a man tested and proven. "But then I'm trackside, mixing in and putting my ear about, as one does, when a familiar voice calls out and up walks Hoy Holyoake, a jockey of my acquaintance."

"Speaks with an Irish accent after three in the morning or his twelfth whisky and water, whichever comes first."

"You know him, then."

"As well as one can a jockey."

"Of course." Pim nodded knowing agreement. "So I'm idly watching the first race, on which I have no investment apart from a token each-way on a filly whose livery happened to match my school tie, when Hoy sidles up and introduces me to this absolute corker of a young stiletta by the name of Charlotte."

"Charlotte. Noted."

"She's a proper cricket bat stunner, Anty."

"Yes, you've made that clear, Uncminster," I assured him. "Try to remember your age."

"It's an important aspect of the story," defended Pim.

"Why?"

"Mitigation," he said. "In case you ever need to repeat it to your mother. You see, when Charlotte wanders off to do whatever it is women do at the races, Hoy tells me to watch out for him on the back of Pickled Farthing in the third because, mark this out, Anty, because his mates — all the other jockeys — are going to let him win."

"Eh? Never," I scoffed. "Why would they do such a thing?"

"To make him look good in front of Charlotte whom, he said, he was going to ask to marry him in the winner's circle."

"Oh, right." I cogitated, briefly, and then delivered my verdict. "Yes, I'd have taken the bet. Probably have pawned Vickers."

"Exactly," enthused Pim before visibly reclaiming his composure. "Then they're at the post, then they're off, all but for Pickled Farthing, but who do you suppose is leading the lot by a length and a half?"

"Three White Socks?"

"Like he had wings," lamented Pim. "But what truly wounds is the betrayal, Anty. You see, I laid my little all on Pickled Farthing with Drafty Weathers, trackside tout and Cheltenham fixture. And as I'm watching Three White Socks positively tear up the final stretch, or rather, as I'm trying to watch him — the animal was a literal blur on the backdrop — who should I see come right up and give Drafty Weathers a sloppy great sweetener right on the lips?"

"Charlotte?"

"Clearly the three of them cooked up this vile conspiracy to clean out my monthly. You think you know a chap and he does something like that." Pim looked down at the blameless button. "So, understandably, I felt Hoy and Pickled Farthing required a reminder of the direction of travel. I chased them out onto the track."

"You chased a horse on Cheltenham Racecourse?"

"With my car."

"Ah."

"You won't tell anyone, will you? Least of all your mother."

"Oh, do come along, Uncle Pim," I objected. "You can hardly tell a cracking tale like that and then say oh, by the way, don't tell anyone. What if I tell everyone I know *except* Mama? Is that a fair compromise?"

"Anty, no one must know."

"Surely someone already does," I pointed out. "Hoy Holyoake, at the very least, not to mention Drafty Weathers, Charlotte, and ten thousand racing enthusiasts."

"We managed to keep my name out of it," said Pim, slyly. "I gave Cheltenham Racecourse my Bentley and they put it about that a sweet little old lady mistook the back stretch for Cheltenham High Street."

"You lost another Bentley?"

"You can see how vital it is that your mother hear nothing of this."

"Yes, very well, Uncle Pim," I acquiesced, "but if you kept it out of the papers and even I didn't hear of it, how is it that Doctor Smick came to know about it?"

"I very much wish I knew the answer to that, Anty." Pim thumbed his lucky button as though it was the glistening blade of an assassin's dagger. "At my 'Regression Interview' Smick just stared at me with that smug omniscience. I stood my ground, but then he took out that blasted file and said 'don't you agree that you'd feel much relieved if we talked about what happened on Saturday?' I suspect he's acquainted with that shameless schemer Drafty Weathers — they have a similar standard of ethics, if a complete absence can be regarded as a standard."

Pim executed another button-toss as an effective parting flourish but then added, "No, Anty, I very much appreciate the offer, but we mustn't interfere with an official investigation. You just leave that odds book where it lies. Oh, good evening, Inspector."

"Mister Pimsloe… Mister Boisjoly."

"Well, mustn't take root." Pim flipped his button one last time and then delivered it home to his waistcoat pocket. "I promised Miss Hackenit a game of yarn skittle after dinner."

"I have weighty intelligence to report, Inspector," I announced when I felt we were sufficiently alone, "Doctor Smick must have disposed of his secret files before confiscating the odds book of Mister Pimsloe."

"That is weighty indeed," countered Ivor. "Because according to Nurse Dalimore the files were in the lockbox this morning — they must have been removed since."

"But Uncle Pim was with Smick when he put the book in the lockbox," I recounted. "And he accompanied the doctor here to the Unladening."

"After which not only did he climb to his sanctuary with the only key in his pocket, all the suspects remained within sight of one another."

"And so," I inventoried, " in addition to an inaccessible treehouse murder…"

"Yes, Mister Boisjoly," conceded Ivor, "we have a locked-box mystery."

CHAPTER ELEVEN

Espionage and Camouflage and a Thames Made Out of Fouettage

The doorway between the dining room and the games room was a wide archway framed with pickets and twine, imbuing a sense of urgency, as though politely but firmly suggesting that passing from one room to the other was something best done at speed.

Nevertheless Colonel Brimble had settled there in no-man's land, recumbent on something that had once been a salon chair made of something that had once been satin and, probably, red. His time had been too much in demand, apparently, to change for dinner and not only was he still in full fishing tuxedo he was still wet from the rain. He idled with the reel of his fishing rod which, for some reason, he carried with him. I pulled up a piano stool.

"What ho, Colonel," I what-hoed. "Not joining the postprandial amusements?"

"Of course I am," replied the colonel distractedly, as he appeared to focus on, of all things, the quoits pin. "It's another rule."

And, indeed, he slowly proved the point as he cranked his reel and drew in a quoits ring, which had been tied to the end of the line. Watching this with impatient disdain was Uncle Pim who was, presumably, waiting for Colonel Brimble to complete his turn. From a seating position — an unorthodox approach even for a game not widely famed for the physical demands placed on players — he tossed the ring. It stopped sharply mid-air and well short of the pin.

"You're not tempted to let out a bit more line, Colonel?" I asked.

"Makes little difference," reported the colonel with military detachment. "The rings are the exact circumference of the pin."

"That must add to the challenge."

"On the contrary," the colonel reeled in his quoits ring, "makes for a fine game. All games should be unwinnable, in keeping with their essential pointlessness."

"Yes, do get on with it, Colonel," urged Uncle Pim from the other side of the field of battle. "I'll give you two-to-one that I can get closest to the pin."

"You carry on, Pimsloe." The colonel nodded sagely from his chair. "I'll observe."

"Talking of observation skills, Colonel," I seized the obvious segue, "did you happen to notice the lockbox that the inspector has with him?"

"Lockbox?" Brimble started and soon abandoned an effort to peer back into the dining room. "No. Is

it a particularly nice lockbox? You should know that my career has been mainly in the military — I've seen many lockboxes."

"It is that in which Doctor Smick kept his files on all his patients," I explained. "You've never seen it? Everyone else seems to have."

"Oh, yes. The one with the files." He made another token turn towards the dining room. "Yes, quite, that's the whatsit."

"You said earlier that you didn't know about the secret files," I reminded him.

"Yes."

"Might one enquire, then, how it is that you recognise the box in which they're kept?"

"Well, they're secret, aren't they — oh, bad luck, Pimsloe — I only said I didn't know about them, because they're meant to be a secret, but now I see you have the lockbox, I suppose they're not secret anymore. Have you, ehm... have you had a look?"

"The inspector and I have reviewed the contents of the box, yes," I prevaricated. "And what do you suppose we found in there about you, Colonel?"

"About me?" he replied with a tone of one resigned to a melancholy. "Nothing at all."

"Doctor Smick didn't discuss the files today? During the Unladening, for example?"

"Not to my recollection."

"And do you recall what he was doing when he arrived here for the Unladening?"

"He was arguing with Mister Pimsloe — My turn, I think, Pimsloe." Colonel Brimble tossed his quoit with less care than one would have thought physically possible. Once again its trajectory was strangled by the leash. Brimble nodded with the satisfaction of a marksman appraising a bull's eye.

"And then when the doctor left, you're quite sure that he went directly up the tree?"

"No." Brimble reeled in his ring. "I stayed here. I didn't go anywhere until the inspector said that I had to go and help with the body."

"Wasn't that several hours?"

"Could well have been. Time passes at a different pace in prison. It was very pleasant to be alone, though. I didn't need to row that boat or play quoits or do much of anything at all. That is, until the inspector came along and made us carry the body. You'd think there'd be people for that, wouldn't you?"

Uncle Pim stood, as one would expect, on the rules, and insisted that the colonel take his turn. I profited from the break in the flow of ideas to stroll over to the tilting fields of pub darts, where Henrietta Hackenit threw for the blue team and Sir Melvin Otterwater for the red.

Otterwater's game was considerably impeded by an evening jacket that looked like it had been provided by the upholstery department of Ferdinand Von Zeppelin. Henrietta, it appeared, was the only one who'd dressed for dinner with consideration to the solemnity of the occasion, and she'd exchanged her grey pinafore dress for a darker grey pinafore dress.

"Ah, Anty..." Sir Melvin lined up his dart with the sober back-and-forth that novices imagine renders them professional darts-throwers, "...what did you make of that porridge, tonight?" He flicked his first dart neatly into the ceiling. "Magnificent, obviously, but I felt it was missing something."

"Flavour?" I proposed.

"You'd say milk, of course, and I'd be the first to point it out, but no..." he launched his second dart directly into the floor perfectly equidistant between him and the board, "...I feel the lack of dairy actually added something to the, oh, the subtlety of the dish, don't you think?"

"I do, in fact, so long as that's some sort of euphemism for bland as sand."

"And did you notice the complete absence of complicating factors like sugar or salt?" Ottewater's third dart, extraordinarily, hit home, wobbled indecisively, and then fell to the floor. "A very intriguing decision on the part of the chef. One which I think worked."

"By chef you mean Nurse Dalimore who, I can personally attest, drinks unfiltered ditchwater and calls it, contrary to any civilised definition of the word and, I expect, several just laws, tea," I testified. "I don't blame her, of course — I believe that she was schooled on the continent — I only state the stark, dark facts as they are."

"Yes…tea…" Pim knotted his brow and pincered his chin. "It's possible the oatmeal wanted for just a little more water."

"Let us agree that it could hardly have made it worse."

"A fair compromise."

"On that subject," I steered, "do you recall Mister Pimsloe and Doctor Smick attempting to achieve an accord when they arrived for the Unladening this afternoon."

"Your uncle was shouting at the doctor."

"This is what I meant," I clarified. "Uncle Pim's take on diplomacy eschews complicating factors, such as courtesy and age-appropriate language. The main thing is, they entered together and nobody left the Unladening until Doctor Smick elected to see out the day in his treehouse."

"Correct."

During this exchange Henrietta Hackenit had taken her turn at the darts board, twice, and missed every throw but the last, which was a bull's eye.

"Your turn, Otters," she announced. "Unless you'd care to call off the bet. We don't either of us seem to be making much headway."

"Were we betting?"

"A penny a point paid on the difference between winner and loser," replied Henny. "What ho, Anty."

"What ho, Henny," I echoed. "I was just firming up a couple of points with Sir Melvin. Do you agree that everyone was in the dining room from the arrival of Doctor Smick and my uncle until the moment the doctor went up his tree."

"In the main," confirmed Henny. "Most of us followed the action into the compound but Colonel Brimble stayed here."

"So I understand," I said. "And is it also the opinion of both of you that no one went to Doctor Smick's lodgings and that he didn't come down from the tree until he was brought down by Inspector Wittersham?"

"Absolutely…" Henny was at once prey to an inspiration. "I say — your uncle gave me two-to-one that Smick would come down before Mister Livesy arrived. I think we can agree that, whatever existential assessment one makes of earthly remains, I won the wager."

"You have my objective backing, as second chair of the Juniper Gentlemen's Club bowls and bereavement handicapping committee."

"Capital," Henny called it. "In any case, that's why Pim and I remained in the compound until Smick announced his gack attack. Livesy arrived just a bit after that but the judge's ruling is final — in a very real sense and certainly by all conventions of gaming and fair play, Smick never came down from the tree."

"I say, Anty…" Otterwater closed the space between the three of us. "I couldn't help but notice that your inspector has the doctor's files with him."

"That is indeed the doctor's case," I confirmed certain facts with the judicious selectivity of a career parliamentarian.

"Think we might get a look sometime soon?" asked Sir Melvin. "I should be very grateful to know — purely to satisfy my curiosity, you understand — who the doctor's spies are in London."

"The doctor has spies in London?"

"Must have. No other way he could have known with such damning detail the extravagant effort and expense I put into breaking my diet." Melvin cast a cautious eye at Nurse Dalimore, who appeared to be expressing serious concerns she had with Ivor's aura. "I once spotted Smick himself at Belle Arome."

"Probably meeting a new patient," I suggested. "Excellent place for recruitment, I'd have thought. I have a clubmate — Elmer Piptree — who keeps a spare suit there, one of two duplicates of the suit in which he plans to be buried. The other is behind the bar at the Juniper. Carnaby has it pressed every year the day before boat race night."

"Rather a coincidence, then, isn't it, that Smick was there the very day I'd commissioned a replica of Tower Bridge in shortbread and chocolate…" For a moment, Sir Melvin drifted into the past. "The Thames was made of zabaglione."

"Perhaps Smick was his own spy, then."

"I think not," differed Melvin. "I mentioned, I believe, that on the occasion of my most recent release, immediately upon return to London, I reserved a private table at Barribault's."

"They have a very well-frequented dining room, Sir Melvin," I pointed out. "Doubtless you were seen."

"For the sake of expediency, I had requested that the table be near the kitchen, you understand."

"Even then…"

"I say *near* the kitchen — it was more what most would describe as *in* the kitchen," confided Sir Melvin. "They set me up on the salad and cold side dish preparation station."

"Perhaps there were other occasions, then," I speculated with, I think, grounds.

"Several, and each dodgier than the last." Sir Melvin withdrew into his sacking, like a turtle retreating into a two-car carapace. "Indeed, only the following night I dined on *homard à l'armoricaine,* baked sea bass with mousse of lemon and tarragon, and grilled pecan-smoked cod, all generously accompanied by shaved new potatoes fried in butter and sea salt and slow-steamed snow peas in olive oil and garlic, with a nearly frozen bottle of Tattinger and a '25 *Sancerre blanc*. What was I talking about?"

"You were saying how odd it was that Smick came to know all that."

"Yes, quite right — you see the entire meal was served in a private dining room, in the middle of the night, in the middle of the English channel."

"For tax reasons?"

"No." Melvin closed his eyes and shook his head slowly and reverently. "Chef Oscar."

"Head chef of HMS Titchfield," I recalled. "I thought he retired to focus on criticising Escoffier in print."

"He did, this was his final voyage."

"Chef Oscar's final crossing of the channel," I uttered in respectful tones. "Then how was it that you were able to secure a private dining room?"

"Yes, well-spotted, Anty." Sir Melvin lowered his voice yet further and Henny and I were compelled to draw deeper into his circle of secrecy and sin. "It was, in fact, his final voyage plus one. I chartered the ship."

"You chartered an ocean-going vessel for one meal?" I stounded. "That must have cost a fortune."

"And even then Chef Oscar wouldn't do his signature anchovy ratatouille," mourned Melvin. "Claimed the aubergine failed to inspire him."

"I can see that."

"No, indeed, I was just disappointed," acknowledged Sir Melvin with admirable munificence. "In any case, once on the continent I realised that I'd spent my monthly and had to get the embassy to float me an operating budget — five hundred pounds, I think it was."

"That seems rather a lot just to get back to England."

"I was in Paris, Anty."

"Of course."

"And, in fact, I spent it all in one night at Maxim's." Melvin frowned into the past. "The chaps at the embassy were quite sniffy the next day, I can tell you that. You can't explain to bureaucrats when you're rebounding from a starvation diet. I had to wire the Home Office but, finally, to make a long story short, I gained three stone in five weeks in Paris."

"Blimey."

"The point is, Anty, that most of my profligacy has been done in private and, for much of it, on distant shores, and yet when I returned to Eden Bliss Paradise Smick had it all in those files of his, along with…" Sir Melvin nodded towards Ivor and the lockbox, "…the names of his informants."

Henrietta, who had been practising a unique underhand darts pitch, took up the point. "I'll give you odds I can tell you exactly who they are."

"Why don't I just pay you to tell me?" proposed Sir Melvin.

"Takes the sport out of it," countered Henny.

"Very well, I've got ten pounds says you don't know who they are. Who are they?"

"Gutter mutters and gossip mongers." Henrietta squinted unmistakable animosity at the box. "I'll bet you anything you like you don't know what they told Smick about me."

"That you gamble?" I guessed.

"You remember last Saint George's Day, when we sailed a flotilla of pedalos to Kingston and liberated the Canbury Park Bandstand in the name of the king?"

"It sounds quite absurd the way the papers reported it," I explained to Sir Melvin. "They characterised it as a drunken ruction by the more harebrained contingent of the Juniper Gentleman's Club for privileged idlers, omitting entirely our initial and clearly stated goal of liberating Guernsey."

"Exactly," seconded Henny.

"Without that key factor, I confess, the entire embarkation describes as very nearly ridiculous," I said, "but take note — the Thames only goes in two directions. Had we chosen correctly history might tell a very different story."

"And you wouldn't believe the tissue of extravagant porkies that Smick's spies reported regarding my movements on the day," added Henny. "I'd bring suit against them, if I could recall the events in any detail. Or in order."

I feel quite confident that my reply to that was going to be erudite and, as determined at a later date, premature, but whatever it was going to be is lost to the ages because in the next instant I was shifted from my moorings, in no mean sense, like a green shoot of Spring that had managed to weedle its way through the gravel between the rails just in time to catch the Brighton Express square on the sniffer.

"You won't mind if I briefly assume your monopoly on Mister Boisjoly," assumed Baroness Garlic as, in passing, she seized my elbow in a grip like the bite of a hungry horse. I noted that she had not so much dressed for dinner as undressed differently — she was in a red silk kimono and from each wrist was suspended roughly four pounds of thoroughbred handicapping weights.

She steered me through the games room in much the same manner in which a chef steers a stirring spoon through weak broth.

"Of all the idle pastimes against which I advise, Mister Boisjoly..." we stopped before the bagatelle table, "...this is the idlest. Bagatelle is the antithesis of productivity. No, wait, there is only one activity more pointless than playing bagatelle, and that is watching bagatelle being played. Yes, that one..."

At, presumably, a safe distance from the rest of the party, which had at any rate entirely lost interest in us, the baroness got down to business.

"Can I trust you, Anty?"

"You can," I assured her. "The fact is I have no talent for the game."

"I see that your inspector has Doctor Smick's lockbox."

"In the fundamentals, that's true," I confirmed, "although I think Inspector Wittersham might object to being referred to as my inspector. I expect he would prefer 'trusted confidant'."

"I need you, Anty, to act in my interests." The baroness released my elbow, which throbbed in celebration, and allowed her glance to dance furtively about the room. It returned with a sly smile. "You must know that I'm in a position to make it worth any effort or — shall we call it — temporary suspension of your normally irreproachable ethical standards."

"You know, Baroness, my father died last year."

"I did know that, yes," she said, with poorly disguised impatience. "Sorry to hear it."

"Among the last things he said to me was something that I shall never forget, something that will always guide me in my life."

"Yes? What is it?"

"He said, 'Don't forget about the Lloyds account'," I recalled. "To this day, Baroness, they're still counting it. In short, I cannot be bought, and even if I could, I would be unaffordable."

"The contents of the lockbox are mine," said Baroness Garlic flatly.

"Did Doctor Smick steal them from you?"

"They're mine and I can prove it."

"Then you needn't meet my exorbitant fee demands," I pointed out. "Why would you have wanted to?"

"The proof is in the box."

"Ah. I see the dilemma. What was this proof?"

"How do you mean, 'was'?"

"I mean to say, what is currently in the box that proves that the contents belong to you?" I neatly rallied.

"A contract, duly signed, by myself and Doctor Smick." The lead weights clanked as she crossed her arms officiously. "It sets out the terms by which I obtain all intellectual property rights of Eden Bliss Paradise."

"And you're quite certain it's in Doctor Smick's files."

"I saw him lock it in there myself last night."

"And is there anything else among the files that concerns you, Baroness?"

"Yes. Everything. It all belongs to me now."

"I mean to say, is there anything in your personal file?"

"Possibly." The baroness shrugged her lips. "Probably. I've got a thick skin, Anty, like an elephant that's seen a thing or two, and my only interest is my interests. No, wait, all I want is that to which I'm entitled, and I'm entitled to everything. Has something happened to the files, Anty?"

"Hmm?"

"There's something in your manner that causes me worry for the state of Doctor Smick's files." The wrist-weights clanked as the baroness put her hands on her hips. "I must insist on seeing them."

"I'll see your request is put to the proper channels, Baroness," I procrastinated. "In fact, I'll discuss it with Vickers right now."

This inspiration came from the heirloom valet himself, who appeared to crave discreet audience with me. We convened by the damp spot.

"I thought you would wish to know, sir," reported Vickers in hushed tones, "that I have recovered the bottle of Glen Glennegie."

"Excellent, Vickers," I whispered back. "Where is it now?"

"In your cabin." Vickers' normally stoic countenance assumed an expression of vicarious injury. "I fear that the cabin in which you found yourself earlier are your quarters. They are also those of myself and Inspector Wittersham."

"Delighted to muck in," I said. "It'll be just like at Eton, just with a good deal less whisky to go 'round."

"I have placed the bottle in your boot box, sir, should you wish to spare the inspector the temptation."

"Yes, most sage, Vickers," I judged it, "and practically philanthropic. The man's continuously on duty."

"Precisely, sir.

"How did you come to find it?" I wondered. "I thought it was buried at the base of a tree."

"By pure chance, sir." Vickers glassy gaze grew glassier still. "When Nurse Dalimore informed me of the accommodations, I returned to our quarters to see if there was something that could be done to make them more comfortable."

"Most commendable, Vickers."

"Thank you, sir," he waived. "En route, I must have taken a wrong turn in the dark."

"It's directly across the compound, isn't it?"

"I believe that my attention was diverted from the path by a distracting recollection."

"Spats, Vickers?"

"No, sir, a whangee," clarified Vickers. "Your father's. It was on an evening much like this that your father cabled me at the house in Kensington, instructing me to bring his bamboo walking stick to the Juniper Club, where he had wagered Sir Ludlow Royce-Phipps and Lord Snowsill-Willit that he could balance it on his nose for the entirety of a performance of God Save The King."

"He couldn't, could he?"

"No, sir, but he systematically believed that he could after a very specific number of gin gimlets."

"I hazard that, on what we shall call the whangee occasion, you took the route through Hyde Park," I guessed, "and that's where you found yourself when you left the dining room earlier this evening."

"By the Albert Memorial," confirmed Vickers. "I found the tree at the Carriage Drive Gate entrance to the park."

"Well, that all makes perfect sense, Vickers," I said. "Except for one remaining puzzle — how did you get the whisky past Diogenes?"

"In fact, the dog was monitoring the periphery of the compound," recalled Vickers. "Recovering the bottle was the work of a moment, and I was able to keep an eye on him the entire time."

"That only introduces a more vexing question, Vickers — it means that you were inside the perimeter when you buried the whisky."

"That's true..." surmised Vickers in detached, smudgy realisation.

"More intriguing still," I continued, "did you not say that there were cigarette ends at the base of the tree?"

"Yes, sir, it's how I recognised it."

"Meaning that someone managed to smuggle and smoke cigarettes within Eden Bliss Paradise," I deduced. "Where was this tree, exactly, Vickers?"

"Near the pond, I believe," Vickers squinted into a rapidly fading five minutes ago, "between the waterline and the sanctuary tree where the murder was committed."

CHAPTER TWELVE

A Chance Glance from the Boisjoly Branch

"Shall we endeavour to preserve the evidence for analysis, Inspector?"

The three of us stood at the base of an ageing but proud Hornbeam tree with a trunk the size of a wine barrel that rose a good dozen sheer feet before twisting off into a tangle of tentacles. On the ground were the remains of three thoroughly smoked cigarettes.

"What sort of analysis did you have in mind?" asked Ivor.

"I assume, Inspector, that you're familiar with the famous monograph on the subject, in which are inventoried the key differences, including grain and cut, of no fewer than nine hundred and eighty-six different kinds of tobacco, which was of such vital importance in achieving a verdict of guilty in the case the papers are calling The Affair of the Maharajah's Ruby."

"Is there such a monograph?"

"I have no idea," I admitted. "It's the sort of question I'd have asked you, frankly."

"Someone's been digging here, too." Ivor bent to examine a bottle-shaped depression.

"Probably a rabbit," I off-handed. "The woods are full of them. Some of them quite enormous, isn't that so, Vickers?"

"Most indubitably, sir."

Ivor collected the cigarettes into his hand and stood to examine them by the blurry moonlight of a misty evening.

"Smoked right to the end," he observed. "Almost no tobacco remaining."

Vickers and I exchanged eyebrow alarms.

"Inspector, you're not thinking of putting the dregs into your pipe and smoking them, of course," I gently encouraged.

The career Scotland Yard inspector raised his eyes from the temptation with a yearning, pleading countenance, like a seminarian who feels he needs just get one more toot out of his system.

"No..." was his weak and eventual but ultimately admirable reply. "No, of course not." Ivor folded the mungy spoils into a page of his jotter and put the lot in an external pocket. "They're comparatively well-preserved. Can't have been here for more than a day."

The inspector inspected the circumference of the tree and then stood with his back to it, facing Doctor Smick's final sanctuary. Beyond that, so at a straight diagonal from where we stood, was the dining room.

"Stood exactly here," he calculated, "I can't see and wouldn't be seen by anyone the other side of Smick's tree." The inspector looked up the tree. "Could you climb that?"

"Do you mean literally me, Inspector?" I asked. "Or someone of my general shape and agility who is willing to climb a tree?"

There were no branches to speak of for the first twelve feet or so, but the bark was of a wrinkly, grippy patina that a determined chap might scale if he were young enough and fit enough and being pursued by a mad dog enough.

"That big branch there might hold a man's weight." Ivor pointed with his cold pipe to a secondary trunk line that rose from the junction. "From there he'd be about even with the treehouse sanctuary, wouldn't you say?"

"I would," I allowed, "although I wouldn't know why I'd be saying it. Why would I be saying it?"

"It's not obvious?"

"No, it isn't," I said. "Unless you're thinking of a blowpipe."

"Well?"

"It's just that it would mean climbing this sheer trunk…" I gestured, helpfully, towards the sheer trunk in question, "…shinnying that dodgy great twig…" I paced out the span beneath the branch, "…and from a distance of some fifty feet, lining up a shot at that tiny treehouse window…" at which I squinted, intimating the inherent difficulties, "…all while being — and I think this is key, Inspector — the kind of chap who takes a rest cure at Eden Bliss Paradise Health Resort."

"Not impossible, though."

"Not, I suppose, in the narrowest of all possible definitions of the word 'impossible', no," I granted. "It would take an extraordinary marksman."

"This is what made me think of it." Ivor positioned himself beneath the branch. "The cigarettes. The killer had to wait for the perfect moment. He employed his time indulging one of the forbidden vices from a position of comparative privacy."

"And the wind?"

"What of it?"

"It's crossing the compound towards the pond," I pointed out. "It would have been doing that earlier today, too, although probably moreso, in anticipation of the storm."

"Challenging, but achievable."

"And how do you resolve for the fact that no one could have done it?" I asked. "Everyone's movements were accounted for."

"We don't know when exactly it happened," argued Ivor. "Babbage only said that it was a fast-acting poison, he didn't say precisely how fast-acting. We need only work out which of them managed to get away from the others and climb this tree."

"With a blowpipe."

"Yes, with a blowpipe."

"Well, as we've come this far on the power of pure imagination, Inspector, I suppose you've also worked out why it was that no poison dart was found in the treehouse."

"I would be very welcoming of your suggestions."

As one does when contemplating the impossible, we looked upwards for inspiration.

"There is something up there," I observed, in a tone suggestive of concession.

"What is it?"

"Sacking?" I suggested. "Or possibly the abandoned nest of a European Larking Mudhatch."

"The which?"

"European Larking Mudhatch," I repeated. "It's a large, nocturnal, cavity-nesting songbird that I just made up."

"I don't see anything," said Ivor with unbecoming dishonesty. There was very clearly something stuffed into a crevice formed where the tree had split with age or lightning-strike.

"Right, very well," I resigned. "You might at least give me a foothold, if I'm going to have to climb a tree to prove a point."

Ivor wedged himself solidly against the trunk and Vickers stood a safe distance. It was the work of a moment to bring to bear the skills I'd acquired climbing fountain sculptures, and within a minute I was scraped and torn and vertiginous.

"The trick to mastering a situation like this," I explained, "is to not look down."

"Yes, Mister Boisjoly, you'll want to avoid looking down," said Ivor from approximately the level of my knees.

I scrabbled onwards and upwards and awkwards. Finally I was able to grip the juncture of branches and breathe and reflect on the perilous impetuosity of youth. Far, far below on the rocky terrain,

Inspector Wittersham gazed up placidly. Vickers, in his worry for the young master, appeared to have become distracted by a vole.

"There is something here, Inspector," I called.

Carefully fitted into the cavity in the tree was a bulbous package in greasy, well-worn paper, but of perhaps greater significance was that upon which my hand fell when I reached for support — a length of pipe. I dared pull myself up until I could see the little plateau formed by the meeting of the branches, and saw a small collection of tools — a wooden box with holes in either side, another length of pipe, and a box of matches.

"Extraordinarily, Inspector, I believe your theory may have some merit," I reported. In that same moment, a hurtle of events overleapt any clue-gathering — first or, perhaps, last, a glimmer of moonlight came to my eye from the high sedge grass on the edge of the pond. Later or, possibly, simultaneously, I observed some very unpackage-like behaviour coming from the package stuffed into the hole in the tree — it was humming. Humming is how the sound struck me in the moment, but it would soon come to pass that it would have been far, far more accurate to describe it as a 'buzzing'.

"Bees," I, for good reason, whispered.

"What kind?" asked Ivor.

"What kind?" I whispered back. "I have no idea. The kind I'm desperately afraid of, I think."

"You're afraid of cheese?"

"Bees."

"Are you saying that there are bees in that beehive?" asked Ivor.

There may have been a slight pause at this point, pregnant with import and resentment.

"You knew it was a beehive?"

"I did." Ivor hid his shame beneath a veneer of indifference. "You made the point, though — the tree can be climbed by a man who is not in peak physical condition."

I was about to object to that slur and back it up with concrete achievement, such as my second-place finish (out of some ninety entrants) in the Juniper kite-flying contest, achieving a personal best of six minutes airborne. The opportunity was arrogated and lost, however, by the community of bees which in that moment sensed that the rain had stopped or that they had a new neighbour or both. However it was, a small but foreboding forward guard popped out of the hive, one by one, like soap bubbles, suggestive of an infinite supply. After a short strategy meeting, they divided the immediate area into searchable sectors and instituted a systematic investigation.

The novice sentries, I felt, were given the more dangerous work. Not for me to say, obviously, but had it been me I'd have reserved the more experienced soldiers for what could be fairly described as the unknown, and allowed the untested and doubtless nervous Other Ranks the largely diplomatic duty of verifying the peaceful intentions of any recently sighted Boisjolys. As it was, though, my quadrant was assigned to a battle-hardened cynic with a torn wing and five legs and a low, resolved rumble to his buzz, like an old battle-bee who has no intention of dying in his sleep.

"Have you a firearm, Inspector?" I hushed discreetly from the side of my mouth.

"Just let go of the branch," suggested Ivor with mad abandon.

"And be dashed to my death on the rocks below?"

The scarred sergeant-major hovered past headquarters in a slow reconnaissance and then disappeared from view where he became merely a nightmarish hum of not what but when. The grinding whir continued, though, and even faded, and then was gone. I felt it safe, finally, to say something jolly and dismissively brave and then begin a slow descent, but then my hand — the one by which I was suspended — was struck on the thin, tendony bit by a white-hot awl swung with meaning by a top-flight professional blacksmith. I released the branch.

The earth beneath the tree, thankfully, was quaggy with wet, and so even from a fall of twelve feet (less the length of one fully-grown Boisjoly) I merely sank into the soil to the tops of my Oxfords. Vickers evinced no emotion but I knew what he was thinking, and so I showed him the swollen great welt on my hand by way of explanation for what, I saw, was going to be a challenging shoeshine.

"We should apply treatment to the injury immediately, sir," advised Vickers.

"We should, I agree," I whimpered bravely, "but first, Inspector, we should endeavour to recover whatever it was I saw up that tree. There was indeed space for a man to sit and smoke and there were signs of someone having done so."

"Doubtless it'll keep until we can construct some rudimentary smoke machine."

"Doubtless it would," I agreed, "but I'm at a loss to know why it should and, as we're touching on the point, I have no notion of the form nor function of that which you call a smoke machine. Is it a device that smokes your pipe for you?"

"It's a manner of generating and distributing a consistent flow of wood smoke," replied Ivor. "The effect is calming to bee colonies."

"I see. And you learned this pertinent fact in the last thirty seconds, did you?"

"I didn't know that you were going to tease the bees, Mister Boisjoly," offered Ivor in weak defence. "Had I suspected that you planned to poke the hive, I'd have obviously advised against it."

"Obviously." I schlucked my shoes from the mire. "In that instance then, Inspector, I shall pursue the course of action advised by Vickers, and seek emergency medical attention." I examined the throbbing wheal that was once a serviceable left hand. "You're a military man, Inspector, what are the usual steps — is it you who proposes me for the Victoria Cross? And then I just wait to hear from the palace, do I?"

"Have we any bee sting medication, Vickers?" I asked when we had returned alone to our leaking earthen hutch.

"Yes, sir." Vickers produced a bottle of Scottish priority-sorter from my boot box.

"Jolly good show, Vickers." I sat on my convalescent bed as the last of the Boisjoly defences set out a teacup and pot of captured rainwater. "Two, I think you'll find, Vickers — if anyone's earned a snouter it's you."

"That's most considerate of you, sir, but I fear that this bottle is all I was able to save," said Vickers like an Englishman. "We must conserve our resources in these difficult times, and your need is much greater."

"All true, Vickers, but for your mathematics," I corrected. "I know where you hid the rest of it."

"Sir?"

"In the sedge grass, by the pond." I accepted a teacup of whisky and water. "I saw it when I was in the tree. You chose well — I doubt it could be seen from anywhere else. How did you get it all past Diogenes?"

"I have no recollection." Vickers drew meditatively on his cup of distilled divinity. "Would you be able to direct me to it at ground level?"

"I would, but I suggest that we leave it where it is, for the moment." I held out my cup for another round of bee sting medicine. "It wouldn't do to openly flout the rules when even Inspector Wittersham is having to go without tobacco. We must flout the rules with stealth and discretion."

CHAPTER THIRTEEN

A Little Fiddle off the Griddle Round the Middle of the Day

"Has Inspector Wittersham's deprivation not accelerated the investigation?" wondered Vickers.

"In a manner of speaking," I realised in the moment. "The inspector appears uniquely motivated. His sense of sarcasm — always mustard-keen, as you know — has been sharpened to a hypodermic by withdrawal, and his stores of patience are reduced to a level unseen since he and the three of us were trapped outside Derby on the Chesterfield junction line, owing to signal failure at Belper."

"I recall." Vickers frowned at and then drank away the distasteful memory.

"Good thing I was there to tell him stories," I reminisced. "You know how the inspector likes my stories, and yet he was heard to audibly sigh earlier today when I was telling him about Erysichthon of Thessaly. Such is his condition, Vickers, that I would be unsurprised if he were to confess to the murder himself. I expect the only thing standing in the way of a summary arrest and execution of my Uncle Pim is your reserve and resource."

Vickers frowned at his drink in that way one — and Vickers in particular — does when one doesn't want to admit that one doesn't know what another one is talking about.

"Your resource," I reminded him, "in thinking of locking Mister Livesy in the feed shed, and your reserve, in calmly doing so. We're essentially marooned here in Epping Forest without him and his giant horse, but if and when we're ever rescued I expect the very next thing Inspector Wittersham will do will be to collar my uncle and hie for the nearest tobacconist."

"Has the inspector grounds to suspect Mister Pimsloe?"

"Not really," I mused. "I mean to say, just before Doctor Smick died by fast-acting poison, Uncle Pim threatened to murder him."

"Mister Pimsloe is known for high and hasty spirits."

"And he had motive," I continued. "Doctor Smick relieved Uncle Pim of his odds book. You know how fond my uncle is of a flutter."

"I do," nodded Vickers. "On one of his recent visits to the house in Kensington, while awaiting you in the drawing room, Mister Pimsloe offered me odds of two-to-one that you would enter via the hall door, as opposed to those of the parlour or dining room."

"Did you soak him?"

"I did, sir. I happened to know that you were already present, sleeping beneath the piano."

"You can never beat home-turf familiarity," I said. "You'd think Uncle Pim would have known that."

"I expect he did, but found the prospect of a sporting speculation irresistible."

"And there you have it," I pointed out with an empty and deserving cup. "Inspector Wittersham has obviously something of the fact that, denied his just punt, Uncle Pim has been known to assault horses."

"And jockeys and track touts."

"And, on at least one occasion that I know of, a mechanical tote board."

"I recall." Vickers topped up our cups as he did so. "He was electrocuted when biting through the wires of the odds board at Sandown."

"Two occasions," I acceded. "Not that Wittersham needs any more of a case against Uncle Pim. I hope he didn't do it, Vickers."

"Your mother will be most disappointed."

"Res acu tetigisti, Vickers, as you so often do. Obviously, we must sift the evidence." I observed, then, that my mutilated hand had ceased, at some point in the conversation, to throb and sear. "The medication appears to be working." I downed the last pearl of whisky in my cup. "Best keep it coming. Drop less rainwater, next time."

As Vickers set about applying first aid I continued the summary.

"Wittersham will have to at least accept that, while Uncle Pim may currently enjoy a marginal lead in the motive and means marathon, it's a close run thing. If nothing else, just about everyone had cause to dislike Doctor Smick."

"Surely not Baroness Garlic," Vickers gave voice to his lively defence of the class system.

"Not on the face of it, no," I conceded. "On the contrary, in fact — the baroness appears to actually enjoy the ice baths and branch flagellations visited upon her by The Smick Method, and furthermore she claims to have entered into a mutually beneficial business arrangement with him, made manifest in a signed contract, sealed in the doctor's document lockbox."

"The contents of which have since gone missing," observed Vickers.

"Potentially putting a bit of a left leg topspin on the claims of the baroness, which have already been placed somewhat in doubt by testimony that, like everyone else, she had some dispute with the doctor, in her case expressed with a stiletto heel." I eyed my empty cup with suspicion. "Did you top up my medicine, Vickers?"

The dispenser examined his own cup and then the bottle. "I don't recall drinking it."

"Nor do I."

"But the bottle appears to be half empty."

"We'd best take some more then, Vickers, before it's all gone."

Vickers continued and so did I, "Sir Melvin Otterwater is the next contestant. He, too, claims to have no disagreement with the doctor and, like the baroness, characterises their relationship as largely beneficial. Doctor Smick's regime manages to undo months of butter and goose fat in a matter of weeks, apparently. So quickly, in fact, that Sir Melvin hasn't time to have his suits taken in."

"He neglects his tailoring?" So flabbered was Vickers' gast that he badly overpoured the rainwater and had to balance it out with whisky.

"He does, and it's even worse than you're imagining," I reluctantly reported. "The man looks like a poorly packed travelling circus."

"Your uncle, the earl of Thistling, is similarly afflicted..."

"The earl of Thistling is my uncle?"

"Once removed, on your mother's side, sir, yes." Vickers finally remembered to hand over the cup of bee sting remedy. "His Lordship faces a similar conundrum caused by chronic gout, a condition considerably aggravated by his drinking."

"No cure, then."

"None that has ever appealed to the earl, no, with the result that his feet are rarely the same size for any three days in a row, and never the same size as each other. So often was he having boots made that it eventually proved more economical to employ a full-time cobbler and purchase a tannery, but he is always presentable, regardless of the weather or occasion."

"Apart from his giant nose."

"Apart from that, yes, sir."

"Still, no one to blame but gout, and gout is a notoriously cold-blooded adversary," I sympathised. "Much like the Epping Bee."

"The similarity is most striking."

"The opposite case would be Henrietta Hackenit," I inventoried. "While all the other inmates have found their specialty, she is more of a generalist, or even a collector of vice and venality. Her only complaint against Smick appears to be that shared by the others — he obliges her, while on the premises, to refrain from all that makes life worth living, and smoking."

"Privation can be a powerful motivating force." Vickers, to quickly counter this very menace, poured us out two more cups of whisky.

"There's something more or, perhaps, less that drives Henny Hackenit. A secret that she's keeping and which she trusted to Doctor Smick." I received my second or, possibly, fifth cup of whisky and water. "She said something this evening, something that conflicted with everything else. Do you recall what it was, Vickers?"

"No, sir."

"Nor do I. Must be this bee sting that's distracting my mind. Top me up, will you Vickers?"

As he did so, I advanced the discussion to "Colonel Brimble. Could idle for England, that chap, and his motive for murder is obvious — without Eden Bliss Paradise Health Resort as an option for his brother-in-law the Bow Street beak, Brimble could simply pay a fine or check into the nick for a quietly punitive fortnight at His Majesty's pleasure. As it is, he's made to come all the way up here and perform backbreaking mimes depicting rowing and fishing."

"Is this not an excessive quantity of suspects for an undersubscribed health resort in a remote part of Epping Forest?" wondered Vickers.

"And we're not yet done. In addition to being extremely unsound on the question of tea, Nurse Dalimore is a woman of deep fervour and unfathomable passions," I said. "She allowed herself to be manoeuvred into admitting that she and Doctor Smick were a spicy item on the menu, although the implication was that the doctor may not have shared that view."

"A man who esteemed his own abilities very highly," wibbled Vickers. "As pride went before, ambition follows…"

"So very true, Vickers." I agreed. "What are we talking about?"

"The deadly Sedgley bins, sir."

"Eh?"

"The seven deadly sins," Vickers revised. "Pride, avarice, lust, envy, gluttony, wrath, and sloth — in the same order, Doctor Smick, Baroness Garlic, Nurse Dalimore, Miss Hackenit, Sir Melvin Otterwater, Mister Pimsloe, and Colonel Brimble."

"That's uncanny, Vickers," I bibbled. "You're right… no you're not. How is Miss Hackenit envy?"

"The observation was intended as a convenient mnemonic for my own use as the conversation progressed." Vickers drew thoughtfully on his cup of whisky. "For some reason I'm finding the thread of events somewhat circuitous."

"Must be the lateness of the hour." I, too, took a studious sip. "You're not far wrong, though, are you? Doctor Smick's entire course of therapy is a salmagundi of flash and fancy, held upright by lashings of unexamined self-esteem. Baroness Garlic, close rival for most prideful, appears to be mainly interested in avariciously mining this rich vein of wellbeing for all it's got. In the case of lust — let us call it passion, for the sake of the analogy — Nurse Dalimore is well cast as the unrequited lover. As for... what was the next sin, Vickers?"

"Envy, sir, which we agreed to attribute to Miss Hackenit, in the absence of a more suitable candidate."

"She is somewhat jealous of her reputation as a loveable rogue and sort of female Anty Boisjoly," I suggested. "Oh, I say."

"Have you recalled what it was that Miss Hackenit said which raised your suspicions?"

"I have not," I lamented, "only that it has something to do with people behaving like Anty Boisjoly. What's next on the naughty list?"

"Gluttony, sir, and Sir Melvin Otterwater."

"By a clean mile," I agreed. "Appearing for wrath, obviously, is Uncle Pim and his incandescent temper, and, finally and unfailingly, Colonel Brimble, the sloth by which real sloths measure success."

"And all equally viable suspects for the murder of Doctor Smick," summarised Vickers with a smoothly subtle hiccough.

"With the exception of Doctor Smick, yes." I emptied what turned out to have been a previously emptied cup. "The others are equally likely to have done it, though, in that no one could have. Uncle Pim and Henrietta Hackenit were in the compound the entire time — perhaps not in each other's direct line of sight the entire time but certainly neither had the opportunity to lie in wait up a tree. Sir Melvin Otterwater has no one to account for his time during the entirety of the afternoon and neither do Colonel Brimble and Nurse Dalimore, but it stands to reason that they'd have been seen by my uncle and/or Miss Hackenit if they'd endeavoured to approach the tree. This is true to a lesser extent of Baroness Garlic, but she was certainly in full sight when the poison was delivered, and she remained beneath the tree until the arrival of Mister Livesy."

"A most vexing problem," to which Vickers prescribed and administered two cups of whisky.

"Furthermore, even if someone had somehow stolen the opportunity, the only vantage point — and then only with a generously expansive interpretation placed on the word 'vantage' — is the bee tree," I said. "And it has bees."

Night was fully upon us, now, and Vickers stoked up the defences of a woodfire.

"Is that fire a bit smokey, Vickers?" I asked. "I'm feeling a bit heady. And cheerful, even by my standards. I wonder why."

"The whisky, possibly?"

"I think I will, actually." I held out my cup and Vickers distributed the remains between us. In the next moment, the door opened and the dewy silhouette of Inspector Wittersham appeared.

"Is there any tea left?" He asked as he loosened the packaging.

"Tea, sir?" Vickers furrowed his brow and drank from his cup.

"Isn't that tea?"

Vickers looked into his cup and then at me.

"Yes, sir," he fibbed. "I'll make another pot."

"If it wouldn't be an imposition."

"With pleasure, sir," trilled Vickers. "A little of what you fancy does you good."

"Eh?" articulated Ivor.

Vickers elaborated in surprisingly good voice,
"I always hold in having it, if you really fancy it
If you fancy it, it's understood.
And suppose it makes you fat?
I don't worry over that
A little of what you fancy does you good."

Ivor's blank gaze lingered on Vickers who smiled bovinely, and then set about making tea.

"Did you discover anything, Inspector?" I distracted.

"No..." Ivor hung the waterproof layer while keeping a suspicious eye on Vickers. "No, not much. I confirmed what we already knew, in the main — everyone had motive and none had opportunity. Babbage, on further examination of the deceased, is standing by the fast-acting poison theory and, while it's true that the tree you climbed was in a blind spot on the compound, Miss Hackenit, your uncle, and Baroness Garlic all claim that no one could have reached it without being seen at any time since the dissolution of the 'Unladening'."

"Excellent," I must have said.

"Eh?"

"I mean to say, ah," I edited. "The Unladening, you say."

"Are you quite all right, Mister Boisjoly?" doubted Ivor.

"Proper Robin Hood, thanks. You?"

"Your hand not still bothering you?"

I raised my hand and examined it for clues.

"Other hand," specified Ivor, "on which you were stung by a bee."

"Ah, that. Practically forgotten, Inspector," I dismissed. "We Boisjolys are made of stern stuff. I was once bitten by an adder, you know."

"Blimey. Where?"

"Where was I bit by an adder, Vickers?"

"Her father's estate in Shropshire," hiccoughed Vickers. "Miss Audi Adder, daughter of Aleric Lord Adder, the eighteenth earl of Slippingford-upon-slipping, bit you on the upper arm on the occasion of her tenth birthday."

"Yes, of course." I smiled at the fond bygone. "Turned out to be a gross misreading of the tale of Beauty and the Beast — she thought that if she bit me when we were both ten I'd have to marry her when we turned eighteen."

"You don't say."

"I often think of what might have been," I whimsied. "But the following summer she released me from the obligation in exchange for my share of watermelon. Extraordinary, isn't it? The lengths some people will go to indulge a craving."

"Sounds to me like a girl with a keen sense of value," sniped, I believe, Ivor's withdrawal symptoms. "We're no further along with the missing files, either — we know that they were in the lockbox this morning, and we know that the lockbox was in Smick's lodgings, and since then either everyone's been together or the doctor's door was under continuous observation."

"Assuming everyone is telling the truth," I pointed out.

"It stands to reason that at least one of them isn't," Ivor pointed back. "However it would take a very broad conspiracy indeed to account for the overlapping impossibilities."

"Everyone does appear to have an interest in those files, though."

"Not the least of whom is your uncle. Thank you, Mister Vickers." Ivor received his cup and sat on his cot. "Mister Pimsloe didn't like to, but he admitted that the files contained very damaging accounts of his activities."

"Particularly if said accounts were to find their way to my mother," I conceded. "Note, however, that whoever took the files left his odds book."

"He might have done that to cover up that it was him who nicked the files." Ivor sipped his tea and then slowly lowered the cup with an eye on Vickers. "I wouldn't normally take it quite so sweet, Mister Vickers. How many spoons did you put in?"

"Twelve." Vickers nodded happily. "I took the liberty, sir, because you looked somewhat fatigued…" By way of further clarifying the point, Vickers sang another refrain from the Victorian music hall songbook,
"Sugary tea and groggery mead is all any chappy surety needs

Exceptin'
Porky pies and corky gin and a smorky pub to have them in..."

Ivor squinted his suspicion at Vickers who, seeing that further explanation was required, added,

"And a little fiddle off the griddle round the middle of the day."

"Are you quite well, Mister Vickers?"

"Sir?"

"He's had a trying evening," I explained. "It's a long way from Thayetmyo."

"Yes," agreed Ivor dubiously. "Yes I suppose it is."

"Sir Melvin Otterwater also admits an open interest in the contents of the files," I veered back onto safe ground, "he believes they would reveal the names of Doctor Smick's spies. That's also true of Henrietta Hackenit, who contends that the files are full of dark libel."

"And the nurse?" asked Ivor. "She strikes me an odd one."

"Nurse Dalimore appears to have no obvious motive for murder or stealing the files," I acknowledged, "unless they're one and the same — she was clearly very fond of the doctor and yet claims that her admiration for him was purely professional. It's not entirely out of the question that the files contain some evidence to the contrary and perhaps the tale of a woman scorned."

"And Colonel Brimble?" wondered Ivor. "Was he also concerned about spies?"

"Not very evidently. He's the only suspect that appears to have had no cause to steal the files. The man appears to have no secrets at all. I think he would regard them a burden."

"Surely that also includes the baroness," said Ivor.

"She says that the files contained a signed agreement between herself and the doctor."

"Exactly," agreed Ivor. "The contract grants her exclusive rights to the name and methods of Eden Bliss Paradise Health Resort. That's the opposite of a motive to murder."

"Assuming the contract exists," I said. "With no Doctor Smick and no files, there remains only the word of the baroness."

"Which I take at face value," said Ivor's reflexive respect for the class system. "Doubtless Mister Livesy will be here tomorrow and we can shift this entire lot to London for a proper inquest." Ivor set his tea on the apple crate nightstand next to his cot. "We'll want to get some sleep and make an early morning of it."

Vickers had been sitting on his own cot, apparently musing on some pleasant thought, when this observation inspired another music hall advisory, to which he gave voice,
If you're sorely or you're poorly or you've got to wake up oorly
There's a simple salve that never dissa-pints
Just a bit of rum and whisky mixed with gin and shaken briskly
A glass of wine and six or seven pints"
and then he fell like a final curtain onto his pillow.

"You can save it for tomorrow, if you wish," said Ivor.

"Sound thinking," I agreed. "Save what?"

"Telling me about the whisky," said Ivor. "I take it you found it."

"Of course not, Inspector. Though, as you mention it, now would be the perfect moment to do so, what with everyone snuggled in their hovels." I bid Ivor a hushed good night and went out into the cloying cool of the Epping mist.

The weary welkin of the weeping day glowed a gloaming purple. Doubtless there was a moon involved. The air was the dew and drifting drizzle of a forest at night, and all around was the tuning orchestra of drips and chirps and cracks and creaks.

The compound presented as a standing stencil against the night, simplified and staged such that all angles were visible at once and there was no place to hide. No blind spots, nowhere to crouch nor climb, no way that anyone could have murdered a man up a tree or made off with his files without being seen. There are insights, I was discovering, offered by the forest and the night and a half-bottle of Scottish science.

Thusly attuned to the void I noticed, for instance, that Diogenes was not in his rain barrel. This struck me as meaningful, and I surveyed the edges of the compound until I spotted the basset hound at the treeline — his head raised, his elephant ears set back, he stood alert on his stubby legs, like a vigilant coffee table.

As I approached I must have stepped on a twig or a beetle and Diogones' swerved a pout of dour disappointment towards me. Then he wagged his head slowly and sorrowfully and returned to his forest vigil.

"What ho, Doggy-knees," I whispered as I joined him at the frontiers of the resort. He raised one cheerless eyebrow in acknowledgement but otherwise continued to stare sadly into the mist and gloom of the woods. I could see nothing of note that couldn't be explained by fireflies or wood nymphs, and heard only the trickle and drip of lingering weather. Diogenes clearly saw something, though, and heard something and, presumably, sensed something subtle on the wind. And then, somehow, so did I.

One of the fireflies flashed brighter and longer than the others, giving meaning to an otherwise innocuous scrape. Someone had struck a match.

"Lead on," I suggested to Diogenes, but he only glanced at me beneath hooded lids, demurred and chose not to explain himself to a young idler who ought to understand — without being told — that a sentry's first duty is to secure the perimeter.

"Wait here," I suggested instead. "I'll investigate."

A dense wood, late at night, after a heavy rain has a magical mien to it, even more so than a dense wood on a sunny day. I'd have been unsurprised, as I picked my way through the clinging undergrowth and stodgy ground and misty, murky, unreal air, to have encountered Hansel and Gretel or Prospero. Instead, as I approached it, the hazy shadow puppet in a tiny clearing clarified into a very corporal Nurse Dalimore, smoking a cigarette.

CHAPTER FOURTEEN

Smick's Smouldering Smearing of Smokers

"What ho, Nurse."

Nurse Dalimore spun like a ballerina, leaving her cigarette hand lingering behind her back. She failed, however, to consider the inevitable exhale, and what had doubtless been intended as a casual off-hand, "Oh, good evening, Mister Boisjoly," instead came at me as though fired from a musket.

"Communing with nature?" I asked.

It was her eyes, in the main, that betrayed the catalogue of claims she was browsing, from sleepwalking to blank denial, before settling on, "Yes."

"Well, there's certainly plenty of it. You'll want to watch out for bees, though."

"It's when the forest dreams that it reveals its true self, and its harmony keeps rhythm with mine." Dalimore recited this to ethereal everywhere. She held that pose for a bit, affording me a furtive glance and determining that I wasn't going anywhere. "And while I was out here, keeping rhythm with the forest, I saw someone — smoking."

"No!"

"Yes! And I found this!" She produced the smouldering cigarette.

"Why, that's uncanny, Nurse Dalimore," I marvelled. "For I, too, found someone out here smoking."

Dalimore regarded the smouldering evidence in her hand. She cocked her head and balanced the odds before finally hoping, "You won't tell anyone..."

"Only Inspector Wittersham."

"But he won't tell anyone."

"Not if I have anything to say about it," I assured her. "And I don't. You might, though, if you were prepared to barter away some of your cache."

"But I have so little."

"How is it, now we've come to it, that you have any at all?"

The nurse medicated on the cigarette wasting away in her hand. Realising, then, that she had nothing else to hide, she luxuriated in a long, deep draw of smoke.

"I smuggled it in," she said, practically in smoke-signals.

"But, how?" I asked. "How did you get it past Diogenes?"

"I didn't, obviously." Dalimore spoke more softly now she'd been reminded of the presence of the border patrol. "Nothing gets past that dog. We're well outside the resort here, though. Last time I came back up from London I brought a small box of Turkish blend, wrapped in oil cloth. Mister Livesy enforces the rules every bit as strictly as the doctor and Diogenes, and so I had to be very careful, but as we approached the resort I just sort of dropped the box off the back of the wagon." She awarded herself a self-satisfied draw of Turkish blend. "Came back that night and hid it properly, and I only ever have one out here, late at night."

"Most intrepid, Nurse," I said. "Have you ever done any espionage? You should consider it, I think, if healthcare and hypocrisy fail to give satisfaction."

"Oh, but Mister Boisjoly, you misunderstand me. I'm very much a believer in Doctor Smick's work and philosophy. It's just, you see…"

"You really like smoking."

"Oh boy, do I." She demonstrated the extent. "I feel sure that if Doctor Smick hadn't harboured such a pronounced bias against tobacco, he might have been able to comprehend how it can connect us to nature." Nurse Dalimore connected deeply and then exhaled a thick cloud of nature.

"I thought that Doctor Smick disliked all vices with generous equanimity."

"Smoking in particular." Nurse Dalimore gazed in sad sympathy at her misunderstood cigarette. "It's why I could never, ever tell him. Anything else he might have forgiven, but if he discovered that I smoked it would have been over between us."

"What, exactly, would have been over between you?"

The nurse looked up with the subtle theatricality of a Buster Keaton double-take. "I mean, of course, our intense and abiding mutual respect."

"Of course."

"And obviously we shared a deep spiritual connection," smoked Dalimore. "We were both Capricorn, you see, and from East Essex."

"I understand that Doctor Smick had entered into an arrangement with Baroness Garlic."

"Purely business," Dalimore was quick to clarify. "The way she puts it, Smick saw the trees, she saw the forest. I recall that particularly because she had me write it down."

The cigarette had burned down to an ember now and the nurse was obliged to squeeze out the last it had to offer between two fingernails that might have been engineered for the task.

An owl hooted and the cigarette, after a short but bright comeback effort, died. Dalimore briefly mourned its passing before disposing of the remains. She then appraised me through the fog before deciding, as most eventually do, to trust me, and she returned her box of Turkish blend to its hidey-hole inside a hollow tree.

"How do you manage to keep track of it?" I asked. "I've yet to meet one I haven't liked, but few of these trees have much of what I'd describe as a distinct personality."

"They're all unique and special, and each one guides me along my journey," explained Dalimore. "Also, the horse trail is exactly sixty-seven paces that way." She began to stride, in that way one does when one expects to be followed, in the other direction. "I find it judicious to take a different route back every night."

I stumbled along next to her, putting my trust in the tree nymphs and Miss Dalimore's cigarette-sourcing sense. To me the terrain remained a hazy, mazey, slightly wavy dreamscape of tall shadows hovering in pervading fog, cast by an elusive moon. Additionally, there was something about my state of mind under the influence of bee balm that rendered every flash and flutter a mischievous pixie with a plan. Presently, though, in a small clearing formed of repressed shrubbery and oppressed branches, an oddly out-of-place obstacle crossed our path.

"What's all this?" Dalimore got to the heart of the question. A rude shelter had been ill-conceived and half-formed of bark and broken shrubbery, made waterproof with a camp blanket roof encrusted with wax. Scattered beneath was an eclectic collection of vessels, including teapots and cups, pillboxes, a bucket, a pewter pocket flask, and a Wellington boot. They were all sealed in an ostentatiously slapdash fashion with wax and kerchiefs or socks.

I peeled the lid away from the teapot and passed it beneath the famously perceptive Boisjoly beak.

"It would be a fermentorium, if that were a word. This is very young mead, made with honey, pond water and yeast gathered from..." I took a slower and deeper breath of the bouquet, "...blackberries."

"Mead?" Dalimore crouched next to me and raised a sealed flower pot like a grail. "Wait here, I'll go back and get some cigarettes to go with it."

"You might want to wait a bit," I advised. "The fermentation process isn't quite complete."

"How long?"

"I'd give it at least six weeks," I judged. "Or, if you want to make sure it's at its absolute best for this sort of thing you'll want to wait, give or take, forever. I thought your vice was tobacco."

"It's accompaniment." Dalimore sniffed her flower pot. "And what could be more natural than mead? You sure it's no good?"

"I doubt it'll do you much harm, unless you're particularly sensitive to disappointment," I said. "Right now it's just sweet yeast water."

The nurse elected to bring her flower pot with her as we continued our trek through the shadows and fog.

We had made a circuit of fully half the compound, such that we exited the treeline across the compound from where I'd left Diogenes and yet, there he was, waiting for us like a housemaster who knew he should never have hoped that this one time the police wouldn't be waiting in the porter's lodge.

Dalimore looked down at the flower pot in her hands.

"It's not mead or anything."

Diogenes met her bluffing smile with raised eyebrows and set snout, expressing glum sarcasm as well as any basset hound could.

"It's just honey and pond water." Nurse Dalimore sat on the grass next to the dog and held out her flower pot for inspection. "Just ask Mister Boisjoly."

Diogenes looked at me and then at Nurse Dalimore and then issued a soft but meaningful "Whuf."

"Shhh!" Dalimore looked around the dark compound, and then whispered, "I mean to say, no need to wake everyone — I won't bring it in." And, instantly making good on her word, she drank the entire contents of the flower pot.

"Oh." It was unclear what she meant by 'oh.' It might have been a sort of simple surmise or it may have been a dawning awareness of the fullness of regrets to come.

"Sticky," she at last deduced, and looked about for something on which to wipe her hands and cheeks. I instinctively reached for my pocket triangle but Diogenes' beach towel ears were within more immediate reach.

His previously pristine lobes now sticky with unripened mead and his opinion of mankind at new and unfathomable depths, Diogenes cast me what I thought or possibly only hoped was a clubbish regard. He then hove about and gambolled back to his rain barrel, wherein he turned three laps before settling his corrugated schnozz on his exaggerated paws and gazing at us in quiet condemnation.

"Well..." Dalimore nodded conclusively. "Now I want a cigarette."

"You feel quite certain that Doctor Smick didn't know about your habit?"

"It's not a habit." She held out a hand for altitudinal assistance. "I regard it more as a ritual."

"Do you have any notion what it was that Doctor Smick wrote in his secret files about you?" I shrewdly posed.

"Nothing, of course." Dalimore affected a preoccupation with knocking bits of twig and mud from the hem of her overcoat. "We were very discreet."

"What about the others?"

"Hasn't the inspector shown you the files?"

"I'm more interested in what opinions you may have formed," I claimed. "My insights constitute the peripheral vision upon which Inspector Wittersham has come to so strongly rely."

"I see." Dalimore demonstrated this assertion with eyes like two monocles. "Well, there's one thing you won't find in the files, Mister Boisjoly — anything about Colonel Brimble."

"Star student, is he?"

"It's not that... the man calling himself Colonel Brimble — I've never seen him before in my life."

❧

"Do you believe her?"

Inspector Wittersham posed this very fair question over a breakfast of porridge and tea, taken in our rooms, such that we might confer in confidence and because there was only so much tea to go around. The three of us sat on our cots like soldiers, our bowls of oatmeal on our knees. It was an ordeal, for in addition to that my bee-sting hand was as red and swollen as ever and, for some reason, I had a mild headache.

"On this particular point, yes, I do," I replied. "I'm not entirely certain how to interpret it, but I believe Nurse Dalimore when she says that she's never before seen the man claiming to be Colonel Brimble."

"And you believe that this distillery in the woods is the work of Brimble as well."

"Not a distillery — mead isn't distilled," I said. "This is one of the characteristics that mark it out for the work of the colonel — it's the absolute minimum possible effort. A still would have required a certain degree of engineering work and the making and maintenance of a fire."

"What's mead, then?"

"An ancient brew of fermented honey," I explained. "Which is point number two — Colonel Brimble's degree from Oxford was in mediaeval agriculture. One of the few skills he'd have taken away from that, apart from the ability to quickly and credibly justify a degree in mediaeval agriculture, would be familiarity with the methods and means of mead."

"Honey, you say." Ivor held up a spoonful of yellow paste.

152

"I was thinking the very same thing," I said. "A spot of honey could take this from merely mundane to positively edible."

"You know where to find some," Ivor reminded me.

"I do," I agreed. "Second floor left of the Hornbeam tree from which one could have waited — smoking cigarettes to calm the bees — for an opportunity to launch a poison dart into the neck of Doctor Smick."

"Can't be a coincidence."

"It could be," I differed. "Did I ever tell you about Will Timmins, chap at my club?"

"Yes."

"No I didn't."

"Why did you ask me then?"

"It was a test — there is no such person." I raised an instructive spoon. "This is a story about another clubmate, Pips Plumbtree, City boffin."

"Yes, now him you've definitely mentioned."

My spoon became quizzical. "I told you the story about Pips Plumbtree and the misdelivered case of confetti?"

"You did, yes."

"Good," I said. "This is a different story. This one is about Pips' extraordinary capacity to read the financial markets.

"Very well," sighed the inspector at both me and a lump of oatmeal that by all appearances had fused with his spoon.

"Pips' remarkable ability came to light quite by chance when Carnaby, our club steward, was overheard thanking him for the advisory to put everything he could afford into a particular commodity because, just as Pips had predicted, the investment had doubled overnight."

"Probably just a lucky guess," guessed Ivor.

"This is what everyone assumed," I agreed, "for, while Pips is as affable as any chap who's ever affed, he isn't famous for his financial wisdom nor, if I'm being coldly candid, any other sort of wisdom. He's actually a sort of genial mascot, in most meetings of mind and reckoning, and often has to be reminded on which side of the players it is safe to stand during darts tourneys."

"Then how did he come to know which stocks would rise?"

"The very question we put to ourselves," I said. "It was Spruce Pinewood who eventually worked it out — Spruce's is a very unimposing guile, and he once in casual conversation got Carnaby to confess to having a first name — what started as yet another debate over how many drops of bitters should be in a champagne cocktail soon revealed that Pips' has an uncle who is considered a big fish in the City markets."

"He had inside knowledge," summarised Ivor.

"Precise, if prosaic," I said. "Nevertheless, the Juniper Investment Committee was instantly formed to put the model to the test, and a delegation approached Pips and solicited his views on a range of active shares, from Amalgamated Puppies to National Eel Mills, or some such things, and Pips very quickly and confidently identified Beccles and Coastal Railways as the stock to watch."

"A railway charter," spotted Ivor. "Hardly likely to break any altitude records."

"That was the generally held view," I recounted. "I think that the collective imagination of this new breed of Juniper gentleman investor was hoping for something more exotic — spice routes to the New World or a synthetic egg or some such — but so thoroughly and uncharacteristically confident was Pips that the syndicate put aside its doubts and risked its little all on whatever portion it could afford of Beccles and Coastal Railways."

"And?"

"I'm not conversant with the measure of these things," I confessed. "But I'm told by those who are that an overnight rise of a hundred and seventy-five percent is considered something between 'performant' and 'honking'."

"Blimey."

"Obviously the syndicate returned to the well and no stock rose like that of Pips Plumbtree's reputation," I continued. "On occasion, he would calmly demur, and advise the consortium to hold the line, but usually he would make a single bold pronouncement on Fiddle Strings Preferred or Federated Fasteners or some such. His cold command was never questioned, the old stock was sold — always just before its price collapsed — the stake was invested in the new favourite which, inevitably, soared to new and dizzying heights."

Ivor who, until that moment, had very convincingly affected an almost total lack of interest in the tale of Pips Plumbtree, levelled on me the jaundiced eye of the seasoned Scotland Yard cynic.

"How much of a stake had this consortium put together?"

"I'm unsure," I replied. "I did not personally participate. My investment strategy is founded on patience and personal engagement, and so most of my discretionary speculative capital is in three to five-year whisky futures. However the syndicate's pool was substantial, and included a contribution from Doolicky Spinney, who once accidentally bought a Derbyshire market town, thinking he was only renting it."

"And these were all comparatively small, inactive share offerings," dogged Ivor.

"They were."

"The stocks went up, Mister Boisjoly, because the syndicate was buying them," concluded Ivor. "That's market manipulation, and it's against the law."

"I know," I said, "but you should have seen how happy it made everyone, particularly poor Pips, who has since gone on to advise fellow Junipers on everything from affairs of the heart to the care and maintenance of market towns. Tricky business, that, or so I'm told."

"How does an uncle in the City qualify anyone and, in particular, one of your clubmates, to advise on matters of the heart?"

"Poise," I replied, manifesting the point. "Pips' newfound credibility in one domain gave him the confidence and calm to pronounce convincingly on others, and to similar effect — Skewbald Runcorn found the courage to propose to Midge Meredith simply because Pips advised him that the time was right, and Elliot Lord Doncaster refrained from telling his father what really happened to the yacht, because Pips told him that the time was not right, and probably never would be."

Drawing on disciplines learned quickly and deeply and forever in the trenches of Belgium, Ivor completely finished his bowl of porridge.

"Has all this anything at all to do with the question at hand?"

"Must it always?" I wondered. "You don't find that a somewhat unnecessarily limiting stipulation? No? Very well, let us examine the tale for relevant insights. Vickers, do you recall what it was you discovered regarding Pips Plumbtree?"

"No, sir," replied Vickers rather reflexively.

"Give it a moment, Inspector," I said as an aside, "I think you'll find the revelation telling."

"Unless, sir, you're referring to the matter of the halibut," twigged Vickers.

"I most certainly am," I assured him.

"Then yes, I do recall purchasing an otherwise excellent fish at Spitalfields, but which had a hook in its mouth," reported Vickers while simultaneously distributing the last of the breakfast tea.

"When I brought it to the attention of the cutter, the owner was summoned from the local pub."

"Rather an over-reaction, wasn't it, Mister Vickers?"

"Not on my part, sir, I assure you," Vickers hastened to clarify. "Mister Boisjoly's name carries considerable weight with the fishmongers at Spitalfields."

"I don't like to put it about — I cherish my reputation for modesty, as you know," I took an unpretentious sip of tea, "but I'm chair of the Juniper halibut and cod committee, a role which carries broad discretionary powers."

"The owner, in an effort to ingratiate himself, allowed it to be known that his nephew was also a member of the Juniper." Vickers neatly set up the punchline, "The fishmonger in question is Plumbtree and co."

"So Pips' uncle, the big fish in the City markets…" tweaked Ivor.

"...is really a big fish market in the city," I completed. "And the commodity in which Pips was initially advising Carnaby to invest was, in fact, mackerel, at six and ha'penny a pound."

"I still fail to see how…" Ivor lowered his brow and his tone and, I expect, his humour. "The fish hook. All that just to draw my attention to the fish hook."

"Well, no, not exclusively that…"

But Ivor was already battening down the slickers and roofing and making for the door. I stood quickly into my shoes while Vickers installed the pursuit fedora, and followed.

The wet was grey with damp and the grey was damp with wet. The rain had ceased hours ago but it stopped and stayed where it was — on the ground and in the grass and on the leaves and hovering horizontal all around us in shifting sheets. The cuffs of our trousers were grassy and wringing before I caught up to Ivor.

"Of course, this still leaves the question of how he managed to get up the tree without anyone spotting him," mulled Ivor as we walked towards the pond. "But I should have seen it sooner — he was even using that fishing rod last night in the games room to retrieve his quoits ring. Obviously, however he managed to snipe Doctor Smick, the poison dart was attached to a fishing line, allowing Colonel Brimble to simply reel it back in."

"Sound reasoning," I agreed. "Certainly he was up that tree at some point, but why do you suppose he did it?"

"Let's ask him," suggested Ivor as we arrived at the water's edge. The forest fable smur and blur continued out over the water where it gained volume and density. Colonel Brimble was already fishing and had quite literally pushed the boat out — he was in the middle of the pond with his back to us, his fishing rod lying lazily over the water chased by the line in a long, lazy arc.

"Colonel Brimble, if you please..." called Ivor. Two ducks flapped in a flurry out of the reeds.

Brimble looked quickly from side to side and then up, a view which held his attention for some considerable time, before he accepted that he was going to have to make the effort to turn around.

"Ah, ahoy, Inspector, Anty," he called and waved, and then pitched face forward out of the boat and into the water, very clearly dead.

CHAPTER FIFTEEN

The Proliferating Pattern of Progressively Potent Poisons

A dead weight splashing face first into the serene surface of a still pond and then floating there, mostly submerged, arms drifting freely, feet hooked over the edge of the boat, communicates an absence of life as fully and faultlessly as a tomb. Colonel Brimble did exactly that, expelling no bubble nor ripple when it could be assumed that even a man of his famous indolence would have made an effort to gasp for breath, had he still any interest in breathing.

Nevertheless, Ivor dashed straight in, discarding his hat and coat along the way. As he waded there was progressively less and less Ivor above the surface, and he arrived at the boat and Brimble's body at roughly mid-lapel. He turned over the colonel and, after a cursory forensic, looked at me and with a turn of the chin expressed a verdict of irretrievable.

"No marks on him." Ivor floated Brimble gently onto the bank. His wide white neck indeed displayed no punctures.

"Were there any darts in the boat, poison or otherwise?"

"I didn't examine the boat, Mister Boisjoly, but that is an excellent point. If you would just go and retrieve the boat..."

"I could do," I agreed, "but only one of us is already wet. And you know the way. Little efficiencies like that can really stack up over the course of an investigation."

Ivor stood with a strongly implied sigh.

"Where are my coat and hat?"

"Did you have a coat and hat?"

Ivor replied with another silent sigh and a bit of a shiver.

"I'm afraid that they were lost at sea," I finally divulged. "Despite my very best efforts."

As Ivor struggled with the boat the first breakfast shift apparently let out. Mister Babbage the coroner, as it turned out, was the first to exit the dining hall onto the compound and notice the singular scene. He tamped down his hat and stamped over to his latest jurisdictional headache.

"What's all this then?"

"Colonel Brimble has left us before his time, Mister Babbage," I reported. "Now aren't you glad you stayed for the second reel?"

"What do you expect me to do with that?" Babbage said from a disdainful distance.

"The absolute bare minimum," I replied. "So we'd best get started. Will you take the shoulders?"

"You don't think I'm carrying a body."

"I can hardly do it myself — he's soaking wet…" From the direction of the pond came a splash and a creative use of the word 'pox'. "And the inspector is otherwise occupied."

Our attention was drawn to the dining hall door as it clapped shut behind Nurse Dalimore and Baroness Garlic.

"Hey, you, nurse," called Babbage. "This fellow needs a hand with a body."

Nurse Dalimore felt it necessary to confirm that Colonel Brimble was, in fact, past saving, before she returned to the dining hall for assistance.

"What happened to him?" asked the baroness.

"He just stopped ticking," I recounted. "Mid-wave. One instant he was greeting us from his trawler and the next he was presenting his passport for inspection at the pearly gates."

Baroness Garlic nodded her approval of the measure. "Live fast if you can, die faster if you can't. Ha!" She scrutinised each of us before saying to Babbage, in a bit of a long shot, "Write that down." Babbage, obviously, didn't.

Presently Nurse Dalimore returned with Henrietta Hackenit, Uncle Pim, and Sir Melvin Otterwater. Pim was wearing the waistcoat with the missing button, I noticed, and Sir Melvin was carrying and eating a bowl of breakfast oatmeal. Henrietta was offering them both odds on a range of causes of death.

While Ivor salvaged the fishing vessel, a party of pallbearers was formed of myself, Uncle Pim, and Sir Melvin. The ladies were excused as was Mister Babbage, such that he might maintain his objectivity. This called for a scientific approach, and so I divided the problem mathematically between us — I led from the bow, Uncle Pim provided motivation astern, and Sir Melvin handled the midship ballast. Consequently, en route to the combination smoking lounge and morgue, poor Colonel Brimble, who soaking wet weighed twice that of a dry Brimble, was dropped on no less than three occasions.

I departed the departed in the care of the county coroner and went to take a wardrobe conference with Ivor in our quarters.

"You should wear swallowtails more often," I encouraged. "It's most becoming."

"I look like an actual swallow," complained Ivor. "What are you doing with full evening dress in the middle of the forest, when it comes to that?"

"I know what you mean," I acknowledged. "Vickers also feels that a classic black silk tuxedo is more adaptable, should a white tie obligation present itself, and of course you're both right, but really, what are the chances of that, here in the middle of the woods?"

"Are you quite sure you have nothing else, Mister Vickers?" Ivor asked in withering desperation.

"Nothing that quite corresponds to your frame, sir," said Vickers. "Mister Boisjoly is marginally taller and considerably slimmer than you are, sir, and I am yet taller and thinner still."

"Yes, very well," resigned Ivor. "Have you anything I can use as a jotter while mine dries out?"

"I have a telegram book, if that would serve, sir."

"I suppose it'll have to, thank you very much, Mister Vickers." Ivor received the book and tested his pencil in it. He appeared disappointed with the results. "Right, let us proceed from the beginning, only now instead of one murder and a case of stolen files, we have three impossible mysteries."

"Two, Inspector," I differed. "The point of the Pips Plumbtree story was never to introduce the theme of fishing lines employed to retrieve poison darts — it was to explain how I worked out what happened to Doctor Smick's secret files."

🐨

"Fast acting poison."

The verdict from Mister Babbage was unsurprising and even, though I wouldn't have said so for anything, a touch predictable.

"How was it delivered?" asked Ivor.

"Poison dart, in all probability." Babbage nodded at the body from his side of a long humidor on which Colonel Brimble's remains lay drying, face down, beneath a poster for Quarter Master Long Grain Pipe Tobacco (natural or rum flavoured).

"When would this have happened?" queried Ivor.

"Hard to say with any precision — a few seconds, maybe as much as a couple of minutes before he died," said Babbage with Babbagian indifference. "And he died about twenty minutes ago."

"I know he did," said Ivor. "We were there, one moment he was alive and, by all appearances, in good health. The next he was dead, and there was no poison dart. What makes you say that there was?"

"Puncture marks," shrugged the coroner. "Clean, deep, and on target. Same as the last one."

"There were no marks on his neck when I brought him ashore."

"Not his neck." Babbage raised the poster above the colonel's immodest beltline. "Gluteus maximus. Two darts, this time. Explains the massive dose."

"How do you conclude there was a massive dose, Mister Babbage?" I asked.

"How do I…" Babbage shook his head in amazement at me. "Have you just arrived? Was that not you standing here not ten seconds ago when the inspector said that the deceased was in good health the moment before he died? Do you imagine mild exposure to a minor irritant can do that?"

"Quite impossible, Mister Babbage," argued Ivor accurately. "There were no darts on the boat."

"He pulled them out and threw them overboard," suggested Babbage.

"Apart from that being ridiculous, Mister Babbage, we'd have seen him do it," countered Ivor. "The poison must have entered his system in another manner."

"If you like," allowed Babbage with characteristic indifference.

"Well?"

"Well what?"

"How did the poison get into his system?"

"Poison darts," said Babbage, as though for the first time. "How did the body get wet?"

"He fell in the water when overcome by the poison," Ivor reported warily.

"There you are then," Babbage took the point. "The darts are at the bottom of the pond." The coroner gazed over our shoulders at a London Underground poster depicting a solitary figure on a dock, surrounded by lake and nature, fishing and smoking an immense cigar. "When is that Livesy getting here to take us back to civilisation?"

"That's an excellent question, Mister Babbage," sympathised Ivor. "I was wondering that very thing myself. It strikes me as most peculiar that he has yet to return."

"I always find the simplest explanation the most likely," I said. "He's probably occupied with other clients or merely locked in a feed shed. Shall we begin with the baroness?"

We found the baroness in the Serenity Salon, hanging upside down like a bat in silk pyjamas.

"It aids in circulation and promotes mental alertness, before you ask," she preempted.

"What does?" I asked anyway. "Silk pyjamas?"

"Baroness, I'm afraid I have to ask you to account for your movements this morning," officiated Ivor.

"I beg your pardon?" replied the baroness.

"I'm very sorry, Lady Garlic, but as you know there's been another death."

"Still can't hear you."

"Ah." Ivor and I squatted.

"Why are you dressed for the opera, Inspector?"

"It aids in circulation," I said.

"Baroness, did you see Colonel Brimble this morning?" asked Ivor.

"Briefly. He was in the dining hall for breakfast. We had porridge."

"Was there anything unusual about the porridge?"

"It was porridge," withered the baroness. "You can't get less unusual than porridge."

"I mean to say, for instance, did the colonel's portion differ in any manner to that of everyone else?" clarified Ivor.

"Not in the least. It all came out of the same cauldron, and we served ourselves."

"How would you describe the colonel this morning?" Ivor poised his pencil over his telegram jotter.

"Fat and lazy." The baroness spread her arms like wings.

"I refer to his state of mind this morning in particular."

The baroness shifted her arms suddenly and in such a fashion as to set herself into a spin.

"He might... have been... a bit more pressed... than usual," said the whirring blur. "He finished before everyone else... which is remarkable on its own... and said he had some important fishing to catch up on." The vortex began to slow. "He was still carrying that fishing rod with him." The spin came to a stop with the baroness facing the wrong way. "No one should dedicate that much time to a hobby, unless it's fishing, to which no time should be dedicated at all."

"Write that down?" I asked on the inspector's behalf.

"No, wait." The baroness cranked herself around to face us. "Hobbies are for filling time that can't be spared. Write *that* down."

The inspector wrote it down. "With respect to the missing files, Baroness…"

"When can I have them, Inspector?" The baroness stretched out her wings in anticipation of another spin. "There are important documents among them."

Ivor, weary of squatting, sat, in my second-best swallowtail tuxedo, on the 'floor' of the Serenity Salon. "You maintain that among them was a signed contract between you and Doctor Smick?"

"Just so."

"I'm afraid we've been unable to retrieve the files, Baroness," I said.

"What? What's happened to them?" With another deft flick, the baroness spun herself the other way. "I knew that… something like this… was bound to happen." As the swirl slowed, she added, "Fortunately, I remember every detail, and with Nurse Dalimore as witness the verbal contract will suffice."

"It certainly would," I said, "if there had ever been a contract in the first place."

"Of course there was a contract." The spin slowed to an apex and then the baroness revolved slowly the other direction. "What are you blithering about?"

"I'm blithering about the seemingly impossible theft of Doctor Smick's files, and explaining how it was done," I blithered. "They never existed in the first place. They were a bluff by Doctor Smick, part of the act he employed to keep his patients believing that he had spies or a sixth sense. You never believed it, of course, because you recognised the cold reading technique from his mind-reading act, when he called himself The Amazing Professor Smick. Inspector Wittersham had no such advantage, so instead I recounted him the tale of Pips Plumbtree. Not the one about the misdelivered confetti — the other one."

"The perfect suspect, I think you'll agree, Inspector." I introduced this theme after we left the baroness twirling, I believe, counter-clockwise.

"With respect to her motive to murder Doctor Smick, I agree." Ivor led us to the middle of the compound where, with much pathos, he took out his pipe. "However she had no opportunity and, of perhaps greater significance, no reason to kill Colonel Brimble."

"Very nearly the perfect suspect, then," I compromised. "Capable, cunning, armed with unlimited platitudes and unafraid to use them."

"If you like." Ivor cast a look of devout disappointment upon his pipe, like a disillusioned parent. "But you know that we have a fully unfailing suspect, don't you?"

"Nurse Dalimore?"

"I respect your talents and your duty to family, Mister Boisjoly, but you must recognise that there's only one suspect that meets all criteria for conviction."

"You really think Mister Babbage capable of murder?"

"I refer, of course," said Ivor, "to your uncle, Postlewick Pimsloe."

CHAPTER SIXTEEN

The Formality of Formerly Waterproof Wittershams

"Why are you wearing swallowtails in the morning, Inspector?"

Uncle Pim posed this perfectly reasonable question from his log chair on his mud terrace overlooking the still steaming pond.

"I was obliged to borrow this from your nephew." Ivor spoke with a flat finality, as though he'd already tired of answering the question.

"Should have asked me." Pim stood and sized up the inspector. "I could have loaned you a simple black tux."

"Oh, I say, Uncle Pim," I introduced the point of order, "did you murder Colonel Brimble and, if so, how?"

"Of course I didn't murder Brimble. Why would I do such a thing?"

"Because he told Doctor Smick about your form book," I replied.

"Did he?"

"He did," I confirmed. "And you knew he did, and we know that you knew he did, because Smick made a note to that effect in his secret file about you."

"Ah." Pim found a waistcoat button he liked and commenced twiddling operations. "Yes, well, that's true, I worked out it was Brimble that told Smick about the book. Hardly reason to kill him though, is it?"

"Not for a normal person, Uncle Pim, no," I agreed. "But for a normal person there's never a reason to punch a horse, either."

Pim twiddled his waistcoat button first one way and then, on consideration, the other. This appeared to provide him some limited inspiration.

"I say, I don't recall mentioning to Smick anything about Colonel Brimble and my odds book."

"You must have done, Uncler," I gaffed, "otherwise how would it have got into his files?"

"Yes, I suppose that's true enough." Pim visited more idle abuse upon his button. "It's astonishing what that man seemed to know. Was there, ehm, anything else in there about me?"

"I think you know what else there is in the files about you, Uncle Pim."

"Yes, quite." Pim smiled weakly at Ivor, whose pencil quivered over the telegraph pad like a sword of Damocles. "There wasn't anything in it, obviously, you must know that. I threaten to murder everyone. How many times have I threatened to kill you, Anty?"

"Seven, if you count your vow to skin with a potting trowel whoever it was who magnetised all your collar studs."

"I knew it."

"Are you admitting, then, Mister Pimsloe, to threatening the lives of both victims?" Ivor put pencil meaningfully to paper.

"Only in the colloquial sense." The button, finally and inevitably, came off in Pim's hand, and so he held it up as though it proved something. "The way one says, as to a valued friend or cherished nephew, 'if it's my last act in this life I shall confirm the colour of your entrails.'" Pim then demonstrated the inherent innocence of the remark by laughing off-key.

"Did you speak to Colonel Brimble this morning, Uncle Pim?" I asked.

"Yes, briefly," said Pim reflectively. "Just long enough to offer him playful odds."

"On what were you proposing to bet?" asked Ivor.

"Not sure I recall, now…"

"You were overheard," I claimed.

"Oh, yes, very well, I gave him odds of three-to-one that I could break his neck for him, given half a chance," said Pim impatiently. "Otherwise our dealings have been quite distant."

"Did you see what the colonel had for breakfast?" asked Ivor.

"Same as the rest of us — damp dust."

"He had nothing else?"

"There was nothing else," recalled Pim. "Quite possibly he meant to catch his breakfast on the pond — it would represent a thoroughly unprecedented burst of initiative on Brimble's part but he did have his fishing rod with him."

Ivor's incrimination pencil quivered over the cable book with the allegro of the hunt or absence of tobacco or, likely as not, both. "Did anyone else leave the dining hall at any time and for any period of time between the departure of Colonel Brimble and when Nurse Hackenit returned to get help transporting the body?"

"No one." Pim shook his head in slow awe of it all. "Terrible business, this. Poor chap." He gazed at the button for a solemn moment. "Out of respect, Anty, don't you think we ought to put ten quid each way on Colonel Quickly in the fifth at Sandown this Saturday?"

❦

"You'll want to be more cautious, Inspector — you barely stepped in that puddle and you missed that patch of muddy clay entirely."

"The entire compound is mud." Ivor looked down at my patent leather flanners. "And anyway they pinch."

"I thought they might," I sympathised, "but my hands were tied. You could hardly wear my Balmoral walking boots with full evening dress."

Ivor raised his gaze with the slow crane of the man with sarcasm on his mind, but in the next moment was distracted, in all probability, for the good.

"Did you leave the door of Doctor Smick's quarters open?"

"No," I replied without looking. "I mean to say, I don't specifically recall closing it, but I think I would remember whether or not I was raised in a barn. Sort of thing that stays with a chap, I expect."

On further investigation, we determined that the door had been subsequently opened by a third party, who was in that moment sitting on Doctor Smick's camp cot, sniffling.

"What ho, Nurse," I said, consolingly. "Touch of hay fever?"

Nurse Dalimore stood, still holding the letter that appeared to have touched off the symptoms.

"Forgive me." Dalimore made an effort to gather together the letters. "I don't know what came over me."

"May I ask the nature of those documents, Nurse?" Ivor was already arming himself with this telegraph jotter and pencil.

"Oh, just trifling correspondence between Doctor Smick and myself." Dalimore flapped the letter in a theatrically offhand manner. "Nothing of any importance."

"I'll have to take a look at them." Ivor extended a hand.

"They're of no significance to your investigation, Inspector." The nurse collated the notes and handed them over. "Very well, if you must know, they're the meagre protestations of a love that transcends the language of lips and literature. Read them, if you must."

"I will," I volunteered. "I'm something of an amateur practitioner of the meagre protestation myself. Might pick up a few pointers. Have you found much to rhyme with 'ankle' without relying too heavily on assonance?"

"Where did these letters come from?" Ivor shuffled them and handed four or five — an approximate half — to me. "They certainly weren't here when Mister Babbage searched yesterday."

"They were hidden..." Dalimore turned and faced the wall, on which hung a copy of De Vinci's Vetruvian Man, annotated for the convenience of the valued customers of Speer's Liniments. "...beneath the floorboards."

"I see." Ivor side-eyed me meaningfully. "Is it not odd that he didn't keep them in the lockbox with his secret files?"

"Oh, no, Inspector. Not odd at all." Dalimore flitted about a bit, as though posing a very real threat of a pirouette arabesque. Instead she turned and faced Ivor, her expression a study in studied sincerity. "These letters, as you can see, are of a personal nature."

"They certainly are, Inspector." I held up one such exhibit. "In this one the doctor says some very frank and fervent things about the patina of Nurse Dalimore's aura. You should probably warn us, Nurse, if these get any more lascivious, if that's possible."

"And in this one he proposes marriage," summarised Ivor.

"That was in reply to my own letter..." the nurse made reference to my share of the correspondence, "...dated fifteenth last, in which I said that I couldn't carry on in secrecy. It wasn't professional. You understand."

"This is odd." I examined both sides of a two-page sonnet Smick had written in ode to Nurse Dalimore's easy manner with the spirits of the forest. "This doesn't very much resemble the doctor's handwriting at all, does it, Inspector?"

"No, now you say it."

"I don't know what you mean to imply," said Nurse Dalimore coolly, "but I should very much like to see the handwriting to which you're comparing it. I'm sure if you contact the doctor's shirtmakers or solicitors in London, they'll provide you with correspondence in that very same hand."

"I'm referring to his secret files," I claimed.

"I defy you to show them to me."

"The bluff, I take it, has failed to catch you out."

"It has."

"Because you know that the doctor's secret files never existed."

"I do." Dalimore tried to pull the emergency brake but 'I do' is such a short stretch of road. "I mean to say, of course not. I know no such thing."

"And the reason any correspondence we might find from Doctor Smick would match this handwriting is that you wrote it all," I held up examples thereof, "Including these."

"Stuff," sniffed Dalimore, "and nonsense."

"He dictated his correspondence to you," I continued. "Just as, in his music hall days, he dictated stage directions to Baroness Garlic's father — Doctor Smick was illiterate. That's why there's not a shred of paper nor anything like a book in the office quarters of a man claiming to be a medical practitioner, and it's why he relied on cold reading and blagging to maintain the illusion and importance of his secret files."

"And I believed you to be a sensitive soul, Mister Boisjoly…"

"Oh, I am," I assured her. "I still get misty when the Vicomte renounces his title at the end of *New Moon,* and I've seen it three times."

"Doctor Smick wrote those letters to me," persisted Dalimore.

"Did he," I doubted. "Then why are they here?"

"Hmm?"

"Why were the letters that Doctor Smick wrote to you hidden in his quarters?" I clarified. "If they were written to you, wouldn't you have them? And how did you manage to find them hidden under the floorboards? There are no floorboards. This floor appears to be formed of rough stone and mould. You wrote them, and then you made yourself conspicuous so that we would catch you with the letters and compel you to admit your affair with Doctor Smick, at which you've been hinting since his departure and my arrival."

One could reasonably expect round, sound reasoning of this quality to be met with a resigned confession or, at the very least, cold defiance. Nurse Dalimore, clearly, hadn't read the rules, and so she instead sat back down on the cot and resumed sniffling. She compounded the low tactic with a full-bodied tear, which I think anyone would call unsporting.

Ivor levelled upon me a regard that was somehow simultaneously blank and judgemental, and carried an implied 'Anything to add, Lancelot?'

"Of course, I don't mean to suggest that you and the doctor weren't very close," I reversed all engines. "He must have relied on your skill and discretion enormously to have hidden his condition so well and for so long."

Dalimore nodded sadly. "I handled all his correspondence." She looked at the letters in my hand. "All of it."

"Perhaps you can help us, then," I said. "Do you know the exact terms of the unique financial relationship that Doctor Smick had with Colonel Brimble?"

CHAPTER SEVENTEEN

Imposters and Spices and the Virtues of Vices

"I don't know who that man was who called himself Colonel Brimble, but the real Colonel Brimble was a patient of Doctor Smick." Nurse Dalimore composed herself and was once again the wide-eyed child of wonder.

"The man calling himself Colonel Brimble was the real Colonel Brimble," I revealed. "The man who came here on his behalf on every previous occasion was, I suspect, the colonel's nephew, Ralph or Edwin or some such. Colonel Brimble told me that he knew that his nephew would make no effort for him without a solid financial arrangement — I expect he knew that because that's exactly what they had each time the colonel was sentenced by his brother-in-law to two weeks at Eden Bliss Paradise."

"He was considerably younger," recalled Dalimore, "and appreciably more energetic."

"It would be difficult not to be," I said. "The colonel didn't have the strength to come all the way to Epping and instead sent his nephew, but on the most recent occasion his wife accompanied him and he had no choice but to serve his entire sentence himself."

"How do you think this relates to his death?" wondered Ivor.

"I feel certain that, had he not been here, he wouldn't have been murdered," I ventured. "Beyond that, I'm unable to say. But would it be correct, Nurse Dalimore, to conclude that Colonel Brimble also had a pecuniary arrangement with Doctor Smick that allowed him to skive off his sentence onto an understudy?"

"It's certainly possible," allowed the nurse. "But if so I knew nothing about it."

"Doubtless he wished to shield you from squalid detail," I said.

We left Nurse Dalimore nodding at this fond fantasy version of Doctor Smick with the intention of putting essentially the same rote questions to Sir Melvin Otterwater when we noticed smoke coming from the bean-tin chimney of the dining hovel.

"What ho, Chef," seemed the thing to say, because at the other end of the dining hall from the door, at the head of the table, behind a veil of steam, Sir Melvin Otterwater stirred the porridge cauldron. On the table were a mise-en-place of forest forage, a chessboard, and a croquet mallet.

"Anty, Inspector…" Melvin raised a wooden paddle from the pot. "Taste this."

"We did our penance this morning," I pleaded.

"This is different — I call it *bouillie à la Epping.* It's got chickweed, chicory, and something damp I found behind the bark of a cedar."

I took up the paddle of goo. "Smells like soap."

"That'll be the violet leaf." Melvin watched me taste a bit before suggesting, "Or the crickets."

I sampled a spoonful. "You can barely taste them."

Melvin looked disappointed. "Too many hawthorn berries, I expect."

"Doubtless."

"Sir Melvin, did you speak to Colonel Brimble this morning at breakfast?" Ivor positioned his telegram pad and pencil.

Melvin reflected on the ceiling, nodded at something he saw there, raised the croquet mallet and brought it decisively down onto the chess board. He then lifted and brushed what appeared to be crushed elderberries into the oatmeal farrago.

"I beg your pardon, Inspector, did you say something?"

"Did you notice anything unusual about Colonel Brimble?"

"Oh, yes, very much so." Melvin bent to scan the bouquet of fragrances. "He was dead."

"I refer to when you saw him prior to that." The inspector spoke with the practised patience of the professional plodder suffering tobacco withdrawal.

"He barely touched his oatmeal, I recall that much." Melvin nodded at the recollection. "And I feel quite certain that he went fishing immediately following breakfast — he had his pole with him."

"Can you say, Sir Melvin, if you'd ever seen Colonel Brimble before this visit to Eden Bliss Paradise," Ivor glanced meaningfully up from a telegram I'd dictated to Vickers, and sent to myself, as a reminder to send Mama a telegram on her birthday, "either here or anywhere else? London, perhaps?"

Melvin was grinding bullrush shoots on the chess board with the rook, and so he missed the full effect of Ivor's subtle ruse. "No, I don't think so. Certainly I'd never seen him here, before, although I understand he was as regular a visitor as this place has."

"Did you not tell Doctor Smick…" Ivor flipped back several pages in the telegraph notebook and referred, I could see from the corner of my eye, to a cable I sent to Steptoe and Giddy of Covent Garden in the name of Dewey Mildenhall, changing his latest order for white dress shirts to magenta, "…that you had cause to believe that Colonel Brimble was an operative in his employ, reporting on your movements?"

Sir Melvin regarded Ivor with a slow, spreading surmise.

"Inspector…" he said tentatively, "…are you wearing swallowtails?"

"If you could answer the question, Sir Melvin."

"Very well, yes — you are wearing swallowtails."

"The question regarding Colonel Brimble spying on you in London."

Melvin slowed his stirring and looked hard thoughts into the middle field.

"What an extraordinary thing…" He looked to me for an opinion. "Would you have said he had it in him? You met the man — he didn't strike me as having the initiative to make a leisurely departure from a burning building. Was it all some sort of act, do you think? A cover for his double life as a perfidious, penny-a-day onion in the trifle?"

"You were unaware?" asked Ivor.

"I was, but it's too late now, in any case, isn't it? Chap's already dead." Melvin returned to stirring the spotted mush.

"You're not tempted to flavour this with a bit of honey, Sir Melvin?" I asked.

"Oh, I say, Anty, capital idea." Melvin raised his paddle and allowed a glob of agglomerate to glop back into the pot. "Do you know where I could find some?"

"I believe I do," I said. "In return, can you tell us where we could find some Henrietta Hackenit?"

Henny Hackenit was, in fact, in the Games Room which, as mentioned, adjoined the dining dungeon. She was playing darts against herself and losing convincingly.

"What ho, Anty." She closed an eye and lined up her first throw of a new game. "What odds will you give me on a bull's eye this next shot?"

"Ten shillings to a penny."

"Done." She launched the dart and missed the board entirely. "Pox. That's a penny I'll owe you. We'll settle up very next knees-up in London."

"If we could just ask you a few questions about your activities this morning, Miss Hackenit," said Ivor.

Henny cast a happy appraisal over Ivor. "I see the investigation has become formal, Inspector."

"I was compelled to borrow a suit of clothes from Mister Boisjoly," said Ivor with a flat delivery that did no justice to the sarcasm, "who apparently didn't have anything more ridiculous that he could spare."

"They're my lucky swallowtails," I added. "It's the very suit I was wearing when I won the Hyde Park to Kensington Gardens Longwater Freestyle. Not the shoes, obviously — patent leather wingtips are wholly ill-suited to freshwater swimming."

"I remember the occasion well." Henny lined up and quickly shot her second blue dart, which bounced off a ceiling beam and scored twenty-nine in cribbage. "You were the bookies' least favourite."

"I was never. Are you quite sure?"

"I was the bookie." Henny's third and final blue dart hit a perfect bull's eye, backwards, and dropped neatly into a fissure between a flagstone and an impressively self-possessed beetle.

"And who, if you can cast your mind back through the haze of poor decisions and folly, was favourite?"

"Spins Purley, I think." Henny scratched her chin with a pensively red dart. "Not by a significant margin, you understand — I was probably offering nine to ten or some such — it's very difficult to judge form in that sort of fixture."

"If I could ask you to return to the question to hand," Ivor withered.

"Oh, right, yes, of course, sorry Inspector," said Henny, duly chastised. "Why *are* you wearing a tuxedo?"

"I refer to the question of Colonel Brimble's apparent poisoning."

"The colonel was poisoned?" Henny looked to me for confirmation. "I thought he drowned."

"The pond is no deeper than the shoulders of a fully-grown Scotland Yard inspector," I pointed out.

"I assumed he fell in and was too lazy to walk to shore."

"A sound theory," I said. "But apparently he had assistance."

"Did you take note of what he ate this morning at breakfast?" asked Ivor.

"Not with what you might call scientific scrutiny, no…" Henny paused to carefully but quickly fire off her first red dart with elaborate English, causing it to miss the board and, in fact, the wall, and sink in the north-west corner pocket of the snooker table, "…but I can tell you that he had porridge, like everyone else, and nothing else, like everyone else. It's all there was."

"Was there anything at all notable in his behaviour?" Ivor readied his telegram book with a morose routine, as though holding little hope for something to write.

"Yes," surprised Henny. "He sat quietly, eating with one hand and holding his fishing pole with the other."

"Was that in some fashion unusual?"

"In this asylum?" said Henny. "Major Otterwater was comparing the porridge to a creme brulé that sparked the ruin of a Soho hotel. Baroness Garlic was telling Nurse Dalimore to write down everything she said and Nurse Dalimore, amazingly, was doing so. Pim was offering odds on you ever making an arrest, and that coroner chappy was taking them."

"Mister Babbage was betting on the murderer?" I agogged.

"At five to one," justified Henny.

"Oh, right then. Fair enough," I said. "What do you think, Inspector? Worth a flutter?"

"I'll do you better, Anty." Henny held up her second and final red dart. "That penny I owe you — double or nothing I get a bull's eye."

"It's a rich purse, Henny, but I'll take it."

And before another nervous heartbeat had passed, Henny hurled the red dart into the very centre of the board.

"You should have asked for better odds," I said. "Talking of which, do you recall what you offered on Spins Purley to win the Kensington Gardens Longwater Freestyle Swim?"

"I don't, I'm afraid, but it was probably quite tight." Henny furled a brow of recollection. "I know *I* was."

"You rather must have been," I agreed. "Most bookmakers wouldn't give Spins odds on winning a swimming heat if he'd been towed by a motorboat. He has mal-de-mer. Seasickness. Although in Spins' case neither word seems fit to purpose. He has mal-de-puddle. He suffers from acute teasickness. Spins Purley is to maritime travel as Hamlet was to stern resolution."

"Yes, I understand, Spins has a severe case." Out of darts, Henny wandered over to the skittle alley yarn basket and selected a yellow mohair.

"Most severe indeed," I confirmed. "He once outbid The National Gallery for Turner's depiction of The Battle of Trafalgar, just to prevent it hanging next to an honoured ancestor, where he might run the risk of looking at a painting which is, I think we can acknowledge, decidedly wavy."

"Yes, I see…"

"Not quite, you don't — the honoured ancestor in question was Admiral Lord Nelson," I said. "There. Now you see."

"Was there a point you were trying to make, Anty?"

"I thought there was." I searched the middle field for inspiration. "Oh, right. Yes. Spins Purley wasn't present at the Kensington Gardens Longwater Swim, and neither were you. You were going by newspaper accounts that confused Spins with

Euchre Cardall. They look nothing alike, but they both somehow don't resemble Lord Curzon in exactly the same fashion. It's uncanny, really."

"Of course I was there." Henny pitched her ball of yellow yarn at the standing skittle pins to little effect.

"No, you weren't," I differed. "In the same way and to the same degree in which you weren't present for the liberation of the Canbury Park Bandstand by the Juniper Gentlemen's Club — it's a gentlemen's club."

"I might have been invited."

"But you weren't. It was a secret mission. No one knew about it, and I mean literally no one had any idea at all until I spotted the pedalos off Richmond dock, where we had convened for sacred club business involving the dunking of Cribbage Digby."

"Doubtless I had the same idea." Henny bobbled a ball of forest green alpaca with affected disinterest. "I'm always doing that sort of thing."

"That's not what Doctor Smick's secret files say about you though, is it?"

"I have no idea what the doctor said about me in his files."

"And yet you tried to innoculate me against them by claiming that they were a tissue of lies," I said. "Both of these can't be true, Henny."

The ball of forest green alpaca struck the front pin with such force that it wobbled slightly. "What do the files say, then?"

"That you have no vices nor addictions," I claimed, "and that your only character flaw is a peculiar jealousy of those who do. You don't smoke, you don't gamble compulsively, you can't tolerate alcohol, and you have a calm and abiding nature."

"Ha, there you go then — nothing but lies. I'd bite your arm off for a smoke or a drink. Show me a smoke or a drink and see if I don't."

"You can have all you can manage, Henny," I said. "My man Vickers returned last night with all the vice a Clydesdale could drag through Epping Forest, and that is a tremendous amount of whisky, tobacco, and civilisation, even by the standards of a Juniper in good standing."

"Where is your man now?"

"Hard to say with Vickers," I confided. "Quite possibly Burma. The treasure of pleasure, however, is hidden in the long grass by the pond. Just follow the dragonflies."

"Right, we'll see who's got no vices..." Henny cannoned a ball of brown chenille at the skittle pins, scattering them in all directions, and then she was gone.

Ivor regarded me beneath a hooded brow.

"You found the tobacco?"

"Did I not mention that?"

"How did Mister Vickers get it past the dog?"

"That's what you want to know, Inspector?" I asked. "Not the blend or cut or pickling agent or whatever it is goes into making a quality tobacco? Your dedication to duty, if that's possible, has impressed me even more than the last time it impressed me, and that's when you had your head in an ice bucket. Vickers got the contraband past Diogenes the same way the killer introduced the poison into the compound — with a confident air."

"How is that possible?"

"Canine distemper," I declared with a confident air. "It can and often does cause permanent loss of olfactory senses which, for a basset hound, is thoroughly traumatic. It would be like you losing your powers of sarcasm. Diogenes lost his sense of smell years ago, as a trainee ratter."

"No, he didn't." Ivor opened the door to the games room, preliminary to returning to the compound. "He knew you had a flask that even you didn't know you had."

183

"Neither of us knew it, Inspector," I said. "With the loss of his most basset of faculties, Diogenes' sense of distrust enhanced to compensate, sharpened by years of disappointing exchanges with humanity. He didn't know I was carrying contraband, he assumed it."

"What about all the other occasions?"

"A refined act." Now finding ourselves in the compound, I manoeuvred the party towards the rain barrel of the dog in question. "A delicate ballet of low expectations and man's constant efforts to meet them. In each instance, Diogenes was only satisfied when the presumed guilty party had surrendered something — a flask, a hawthorn berry, an entire sulky wagon of quail eggs, Iberian ham, roast pheasant, port pies, and Bollinger's."

"And pipe tobacco."

"And, as you say, pipe tobacco," I confirmed. "We all assumed it was his extraordinary sense of smell and not his even more extraordinary pessimism at work, but then Vickers got a bottle of whisky past him and, it turned out, all of the contraband."

"I thought you said that Mister Vickers had hidden everything in the high grass by the pond."

"Yes, I did say that, didn't I?" I recalled. "I spotted it when I was in the bee tree. Doubtless this was done after the encounter with the tiger from which, incidentally, Vickers was saved not by Diogenes' sense of smell but his acute hearing. He has enormous ears, which, I will ask you to observe, have another unique quality."

"Is that lipstick?"

"Cérise Venasque," I guessed, accurately, "along with a bit of mead, both provided by Nurse Dalimore. Notice anything else?"

"No."

"Exactly, Inspector. Unlike Baguette the Talking Dog and certainly unlike any other basset who lives in a muddy compound,

Diogenes has clean ears. This is because, distinguishing him from other members of his noble breed, he doesn't go about with his nose to the ground. It was this observation which first made me suspect that of which I'm now certain — Diogenes has no sense of smell, and someone in Eden Bliss Paradise Health Resort — besides myself, I mean — knows it."

As if to illustrate the point, Diogenes raised his oversized head and frowned at something unseen in the morning mist which still loitered in strands in the compound and sulked in shrouds in the forest.

"Wuf," said the dog, authoritatively.

The forest fog rippled and flowed but in the main presented a solid screen onto which, presently, was cast an enormous silhouette. Diogenes leapt to his feet and breathed a low 'Stand back, I'll handle this,' and approached the monstrosity, which stirred and snorted and loomed in the obscurity.

In the next instant, the monster whinnied, the fog cleared, and standing clear and huge was Mister Livesy's Clydesdale, and next to him, breathing stentoriously through a curled lip, was Mister Livesy.

CHAPTER EIGHTEEN

Poisonous Plans for Banned Contraband

"Where is that Mister Vickers," Mister Livesy wanted to know. He had changed little since last viewed, and was still in overalls and cloth cap, free-roaming whiskers and magnificent eyebrows, but he had acquired a distinctly oatmealy quality.

"Ah, Mister Livesy," I stalled. "Vickers will be most gratified to see you and your giant horse. When he told me what happened we were all stunned that such a thing could occur."

"What thing?" Mister Livesy had about him a sceptical quality which I felt to be unfounded.

"Yes, what a thing indeed," I piffled.

"He locked me in the feed shed."

"Ah, now, he thought you might think that," I said. "Of course Vickers didn't lock you in the feed shed. The horse did."

"The horse."

"That one, right there."

"Clyde locked me in the feed shed." Livesy, if anything, sounded only more doubtful.

"Is that his name?" I dallied. "Very fitting. Not wildly imaginative, of course, but I'll bet he never forgets it."

"You were telling me how my horse locked me in the feed shed," Livesy helpfully reminded.

"Something — we suspect a bat — startled him," I explained. "A bat flew out of the feed shed just as you went in, Vickers tells me, and this put the wind up Clyde something fierce. He kicked up, lodging some sort of farm implement..."

"A pitchfork."

"Ah, Vickers said he thought it was a pitchford, but I said, what use would a pitchfork be with oats? I must tell him that he was correct. Whatever it was, Clyde managed to lodge it against the door of the feed shed."

"And so Mister Vickers just left me there."

"Well, there wasn't time, was there?" I extemporised. "Clyde was spooked and he remained spooked, and he dashed madly off into the forest. Vickers — first asking himself, no doubt, what would Mister Livesy do in these circumstances — followed."

"He followed Clyde into the forest." Livesy had a knack for the dubious summation and probably could have, were he not so eminent in whatever it was his field was, have been a very effective King's counsel, the chief skill of which, in my experience, is an infectious doubt.

"Vickers is a talented and tested tracker," I said. "His experiences, however, are largely restricted to Southeast Asia, the terrain and, most particularly, flora of which, he tells me, differ sharply from that of Epping Forest. He was soon lost."

The forest itself replied to this with a low, admonitory grumble. Livesy and Clyde and I looked up but Ivor settled upon me a judgemental gaze from beneath a censorious brow. A herald wind grew in a flurry and fury through the leaves, giving short warning that not only was a storm coming but, in that way of densely canopied woods, it had already arrived.

"I propose that we take shelter in the dining hall where, Mister Livesy, there is an abundance of oatmeal porridge," I said. "Vickers insisted."

We installed Clyde the Clydesdale and his sulky carriage beneath the firewood shelter. Diogenes, after a tour of the perimeter, returned to his rain barrel. Ivor, Livesy, and I joined Sir

Melvin Otterwater in the dining hall. Now having completed his experiments, Sir Melvin sat like a pantomime goldilocks with a dozen bowls of subtle variations on the theme of porridge.

"Oh." Sir Melvin regarded Boisjoly, party of three. "There's really not enough to go 'round." He ran a finger around the inside of a bowl and ate the remnants. "And I'm afraid that's the last of the oatmeal."

"Doubtless Mister Livesy has brought more," I said.

"I've done nothing of the kind," objected Mister Livesy.

"Then what's all that sacking on Clyde's sulky?" I was asking when the door opened again and Baroness Garlic and Nurse Dalimore entered, mid-platitude.

"If you blame some man for your unhappiness then it means you're in his debt when you're happy," expounded the baroness. "No, wait… actually, no, don't wait. Write that down."

Nurse Dalimore didn't write it down, but she did nod an unmistakable 'you betcha'. This was accompanied by a long, low trundle of corroborating thunder.

"There's a storm coming," announced the baroness. "Ideal weather for a natural dip in the pond. Excellent for the pores."

"We'll remain here for the duration, I think, Baroness," Ivor was quick to say. "And indeed, now that Mister Livesy has arrived, I think that we should all prepare to leave."

"Livesy!" exclaimed, on first impressions, the door. It turned out to be Babbage, however, who had come through at that moment and recognised his lifeline. "Let's go."

It was at this moment, with the door open wide on the compound and treeline beyond, that the long-approaching tempest made landfall in the form of a solid pipe of rain the length and width of Eden Bliss Paradise Health Resort.

"I'm not going out in this," declared Mister Livesy, who had edged his way towards the kettle fire.

Uncle Pim, being of a similar mind, splashed through the door. "It's pelting." He pushed the door closed behind him. "I'll give anyone four-to-three it lasts all day."

"I'll give you ten pounds to take me to a tobacconist," Babbage said to Livesy.

"We'll have to make arrangements for the transport of the bodies, first and foremost, Mister Babbage." Ivor spoke with authority but I could see him fiddling with his pipe in his pocket.

"That won't save a minute of anyone's time," Babbage assured him. "Because if I'm not inhaling the issue of a quality cigar in the next hour I'm going to murder someone." The coroner pulled off his hat as he spoke and squinted defiantly at Ivor. Finally the stare broke. "Why are you wearing a tuxedo?"

The door opened yet again and Vickers came through beneath a broad umbrella. He pirouetted like a lifetime valerina, shook out the brolly and, when he turned back to the room, was dry and dignified.

"I have brought tea, sir."

"Real tea?" wondered just about everyone.

"I'd like a word with you, if you don't mind, Mister Vickers," said Livesy.

"Certainly, sir. "Vickers betrayed no indication that he recognised Mister Livesy. "But first, if I failed to mention it, I have brought tea."

Vickers set about the fire and metal with tea and kettle and the storm set about the roof of the dining hall with a biblical fury.

"This strikes me the ideal moment in which to review the state of affairs," I proposed. "Just about all the suspects are on hand, there's an accompanying storm and a cosy fire, and any minute now there'll be tea."

"Miss Hackenit's not here," pointed out the inspector.

"I expect she's out proving a point," I speculated. "Or, more probably, failing to do so. Doubtless she'll be along presently. We can leave her to last."

"Last what?" Baroness Garlic wanted to know.

"Last suspect," I replied followed, in a sort of aside, "Thank you, Vickers," as I received my cup of warm weather-beater. "You can be first, if you like, Baroness."

"Do your worst, Boisjoly."

"I always do, Your Ladyship," I assured her. "As established, you had no agreement with Doctor Smick, but you claimed that you did."

"It was verbal."

"And yet just before he died you threatened him with a stiletto shoe."

"It's a very common negotiating tactic." The Baroness turned away to sip her tea in the manner of the explicitly not bothered. "Anyone in business will tell you that."

"But you said that the contract was signed, Baroness," I reminded her. "If that were so, there would have been nothing left to negotiate."

"Then what would have been the point in killing him?"

"You knew there were no secret files," I explained. "You hoped that with the doctor deceased and in the absence of a signed contract, you could recall whatever terms you wished."

The baroness regarded me casually over her cup. "I still had no reason to kill Colonel Brimble. I barely knew the man."

"Did anyone know Colonel Brimble?" Ivor set down his tea to withdraw his telegraph jotter. "Sir Melvin?"

"He was a spy in the employ of Doctor Smick," replied Sir Melvin distractedly.

"How do you come to know that?"

190

"Why, you told me, Inspector." Sir Melvin looked to me for support. "About an hour ago."

"We were speculating," I said. "Nevertheless, you did have cause to murder Doctor Smick."

"Oh, yes," agreed Sir Melvin. "To know him was to have cause to murder him."

"But again, no reason to kill Colonel Brimble," lamented Ivor.

"The spying thing," offered Sir Melvin.

"None that you actually knew about," I clarified. "In any case, I doubt very much that Colonel Brimble had the initiative for covert surveillance, despite the coincidence of his presence at Belle Arome."

"Another suspect with middling motive for the first murder." Ivor sifted his scant telegraph notes. "And none at all for the second."

A sweep of wind brushed a flush of rain across the roof of earth and wood and gaping holes. This was accompanied by a grumble of thunder that seemed to rumble at odds with Ivor's contention. We all looked up, as one does, and saw only darkness and wet slipping through the holes in the roof.

Nurse Dalimore, I noted, was savouring real tea as though it was a particularly well-brewed cup of ambrosia. She took notice of my taking notice, and mounted a defence.

"Well I certainly had no cause to murder Doctor Smick."

"Unrequited love is often taken to be a motive," I said. "Not by me, obviously — I regard rejection as character-building, like working out the electric bill, although with greater frequency, obviously."

"He never rejected me." Dalimore hugged her cup of tea defiantly. "We were in love, and I don't care who knows it."

"Yes, you do," I differed. "You want everyone to know it. It's why you wrote both ends of the romantic correspondence that you then pretended to find in Smick's quarters."

Dalimore looked at something sad in her cup. The rain sympathised in a heavy hum on the roof and steady drip on the floor.

"He still loved me, though. He just couldn't express it in writing, so I did it for him."

"In any case," Ivor said, mainly to me, "still no motive for the second murder."

"I say, Anty, what about Henny?" asked Uncle Pim.

"A fair question," I judged it. "What about her? Well, it turns out her one and only vice is a profound jealousy of those of us with vices, to the point of affecting to suffer from them all. Like that chap, what was his name, Vickers? Followed me down from Eton one summer and absolutely idolised me. Did everything I did in minute detail, up to and including getting jugged for impersonating a bishop."

"You're thinking of His Highness Prince Henry, sir, The Duke of Gloucester," supplied Vickers.

"That's the chappy. What a cipher."

"Henny's not a gambler?" marvelled Pim.

"Nor a drinker nor a smoker," I said. "Probably keeps a household journal and rises early on the weekends."

"Not like you, Anty, to speak ill of those not present." Pim abstractedly abused a button of his waistcoat. "And, in fact, it is to this point that I referred when I asked after her. Where is she?"

"Seeking validation, I believe," I guessed. "But all she'll prove, either way, is that she had reason to resent Doctor Smick, although, once again, she had nothing against Colonel Brimble."

"None of us did," claimed Baroness Garlic.

"He was never even here," added Nurse Dalimore.

"That's true. Not only was he an entirely innocuous presence, he was very rarely even present," I agreed. "Even the time he spent here was served by a stand-in. There was one among us, though, and only one, who had a quarrel with both victims. Isn't that so, Uncle Pim?"

"I didn't kill anyone, Anty, you know me better than that."

"You once threatened to drown me in the bird bath."

"You were cheating at croquet."

"I was four years old, Uncling, and I still believe you made up that rule forbidding barn owl impersonations during an opponent's turn."

"Can I presume, then, Mister Boisjoly, that you've worked out how the murders were committed, and by whom?" asked Ivor, his pencil poised to take a telegram.

I hated to disappoint. We had everyone gathered with no place to go and there was a crashing great storm outside, but in the absence of an inspiration within the next minute or so I was going to have to levy the bad news.

"I'm afraid not, Inspector," I levied. "I still have no idea how the murders were committed."

Probably for the best, the dark moment was broken by an explosion of thunder that shook some mould loose from the ceiling. One of the drips became a steady stream, and two new leaks opened up.

"I believe it's clearing up." Babbage, who found himself directly beneath one of the new leaks, put on his hat. "Shall we be going, Mister Livesy?"

"Eh?" Livesy bristled his brow at Babbage. "Are you mad? There's no going anywhere in this. Clyde would sink to his ears. What do you want to be going out in this weather for?"

"You look like a reasonable man, Mister Livesy," poised Babbage, "but looks, very apparently, can be deceiving. Even illusory. Of course I don't want to go out in this tempest. If what I wanted was to be standing in a torrential storm, I would hardly need to remain here bandying nonsense with you, would I? What I want, Mister Livesy, is a smoke."

"Well, then, curse you, just go and get the tobacco off the sulky," countered Mister Livesy. "If you think I'm doing it you're as mad as you look standing under a leak with a bowler hat."

"Are you saying that there's tobacco on that carriage, Mister Livesy?" Ivor appeared, if anything, more intrigued than was Mister Babbage.

"It's loaded with all manner of filth," answered Livesy. "Tobacco, champagne, little eggs..."

"Quail eggs?" I said, coming into the terrifying light.

"Pork pies, roast pheasant..."

"Mister Livesy, if I may, where did you find Clyde?"

"In the woods."

"Still loaded with all that Vickers had brought," I surmised.

"Pure poison," said Livesy. "What you lot want is some oatmeal."

And there it was. The missing inspiration that explained all.

"Inspector, I now know how the murders were committed," I said. "What's more, a third death is imminent unless we act swiftly and, indeed, it may already be too late."

"You've worked out who did it?"

"I already knew who did it, Inspector," I reported as I made for the door. "Sir Melvin Otterwater is responsible for both deaths."

CHAPTER NINETEEN

Eden Bliss Paradise and Everything Vise

"We must find Henrietta Hackenit." I addressed the assembly from the open door, the crashing storm at my back. "She's out there with poisoned cigarettes and whisky, attempting to prove that she's a slave to both. Everyone must split up and search the other buildings. The inspector and I will go to the cache of contraband."

Ivor and I splashed across the compound and slid and slithered to the banks of the pond. Slowed by the mud, we eventually made our way to the long sedge grass and the spot I thought Vickers had chosen to hide the treasure. The grass was flattened and there were signs of hastily unwrapped parcels, but Henny was gone, and so were the whisky and tobacco.

"She'll be in her quarters," Ivor shouted over the storm, but when we returned to the compound the entire search party — including Sir Melvin Otterwater — reported no results.

"Inspector…" I scanned the forest edge, a splintered screen behind the driving rain. "What have I done?"

"We'll find her, Boisjoly." Ivor withdrew his pipe of command and addressed the troops. "Miss Hackenit is somewhere in the woods. We need to spread the search in all directions starting from the compound. Off you go."

Everyone splashed off in all directions. I drew due east or, at any rate, the way that took me past Diogenes' rain barrel. I called to him but he was somehow already aware of the urgency and emergency — he tottered on ahead, employing his giant paws on the mud like snowshoes.

Then we were in the woods and all directions were the same. The splitting summer sky roared and rattled and flashed astral

195

pyrotechnics behind roiling, folding, wringing purple clouds, emptying their quivering spleens on Epping Wood. I followed Diogenes through the thrum and chaos but we might have been running in circles for all I knew and, certainly, for all the progress we were making in marking the parts of the forest where Henrietta Hackenit was not. I might have been standing right next to her.

There was, though, something in Diogenes' deliberate, dogged, darting between the trees off which I bounced that gave me the faith to follow. Intermittently and for only a moment he'd stop and get his bearings, squinting against the rails of rain. Then he'd adjust course and once again lead into the boiling heart of the storm.

Finally he stopped, hidden but for his oversized head by fallen logs and undergrowth. He quickly shook such that his ears flapped away spectacular spirals of water. He cocked his head and listened through what for me was a single, hissing note. But then, unlike Diogenes, I detected something on the air, something that penetrated even the solid state of wet — the ill wind of the factory-made cigarette. As Henny smoked I calculated how much time we had left to save her, working with the single variable that Babbage had provided — fast-acting poison.

In that same instant, Diogenes disappeared, swallowed by the brush and briar. I turned in a frenzy and finally saw the undergrowth flowing in a southerly direction, as though in the wake of a great shark. I bolted to follow and then disappeared myself, my foot stirruped in a root. From the cover of shrubbery I thought I could hear what Diogenes heard — the sound of a call for help. This was presently joined by a deep, clear, carrying 'woof'.

Ivor and I broke through the curtain of weather in the same moment to find Sir Melvin Otterwater, who had been hailing us through the storm, and Diogenes standing by the rudimentary shelter over the mead fermentorium. Sitting beneath it, dry and exactly as alive as she'd been when last seen, was Henrietta

Hackenit, prodding a fire of factory-made cigarettes with an empty whisky bottle.

❦

"Very well, Anty, you're right." Henrietta huddled beneath a horse blanket by the fire in the dining hall. "I dumped out all the whisky too, I'm afraid. I was staging it to look as though I'd had the lot."

The storm continued to thump the roof and the wind continued to try to pry it off altogether. We all gathered around the fire, dripping and drying and awaiting relief.

"Well, of course I'm right," I reluctantly conceded. "I had it all worked out by the third time you claimed to have been on a toot that was closed to all but members of the Juniper Gentleman's Club. You were living vicariously through newspaper slurs and libels and uncannily accurate accounting of the events in question. What I haven't entirely worked out is why."

Henny plucked distractedly at her horse blanket. "It's just, I've lived such a sheltered life. I was raised by a maiden aunt, you see. I'd never seen London until I was of age, and the only accounts I had to go by were the society pages that, for some reason, my aunt allowed into the house. She hoarded them, in fact, in particular anything to do with you."

"Me?"

"Well, no, in point of fact, not specifically, but they somehow always turned out to be about you, in the main." Henny furrowed a brow with that plough for a moment. "Well, at any rate, I positively burned with jealousy. The closest I ever came to getting arrested for causing a drunken disturbance was at the village fête when I went a dozen-too-many times around the maypole, got dizzy, and fell into the pluck-a-duck pool, taking the parson with

197

me. It was on the front page of the Upper Bedding Shopper for two weeks."

"Something very similar happened to me, at a fête in Fray," I recalled, "except instead of a parson it was the Bishop of Basildon, and instead of the pluck-a-duck pool I sank a barge."

"Well, there you go." Henny presented me like damning evidence. "It's always just too, too rakish and fun to be an idling waster."

"Take note, young Henrietta, the papers only report the highlights," I cautioned. "They won't tell you about the long hours and exhausting gala evenings at the palace."

"I'll have to take your word on that." Henny opened her horse blanket to reveal and regard her smock dress with puffy shoulders and lace borders. "I made all these racy frocks and went to London and just waited and nothing happened. No one invited me to a lock-in party at The Criterion or to climb onto the roof of Hotham House on Boat Race Night. I could hardly go to the courses or casinos alone, and no one ever asked me and I didn't have anyone to ask."

"Not even your old school chums?"

"I was privately educated. By spinsters."

"Ah."

"And then when I'd go back to Upper Bedding, of course I couldn't say that I spent my time in London loitering at the library and the National Gallery." Henny flattened a plait on her pinafore apron. "So, obviously, I just recounted tales from the society pages, starting with the occasion on which you and I and the cast of *No, No, Nanette* organised a steeple chase of pantomime horses through Covent Garden market."

"I remember it well," I recalled. "The back end of Cinderella's draft horse did it in a walk-over at three-to-two."

"And things carried on along those lines," continued Henny. "Everyone believed that I was quaffing of the cup of life and, frankly, that neatly fit the bill. I could tell the tales without paying the consequences — that is, until my aunt decided that I was on the road to ruin and she sent me to Eden Bliss Paradise to filter out the smoke and sin."

"And once here, you continued the ruse," I surmised.

"I could hardly tell the truth, could I? Doctor Smick seemed to see right through the act, though, initially. Now, of course, I realise that he was doing an act of his own."

"Which is why you said that his secret files were nothing but scurrilous accusations of regular habits and sound judgement."

"And it's why I burned all the cigarettes and dumped the whisky," confirmed Henny. "It was all part of the act."

I waited for a barrel of thunder to roll past. "And it was a most compelling performance, but to be entirely convincing you'd have needed to do appreciably less breathing. The cigarettes and whisky were heavily poisoned. Nicotine would be my guess, but doubtless Sir Melvin can provide."

"Hm?" Sir Melvin's attention had been focused on the door. "Oh, yes, nicotine in the whisky, arsenic in the cigarettes. I felt the balance of flavours would be more subtle while maintaining a certain originality. Ah!"

The door opened then and Vickers swept in from the roar and rush of the storm. He carried with him promising baskets and boxes and bags of treasure from the distant, exotic markets of Kensington and Camden.

"Where did you get all that, then?" Mister Livesy wanted to know in a distinctly spoil-sporty tone of voice.

"Vickers is acting on my authority, Mister Livesy," I said. "The women are weak with hunger and the children are weary and the men are snippy, and so Vickers has recovered emergency rations from Clyde's carriage."

"And you can take it right back." Livesy squelched into position between the dining table and Vickers, thumbs twined resolutely into lapels.

"Surely, Mister Livesy, you can see how great is our need," I pointed out, "not to mention that you're hopelessly outnumbered."

"Not planning on returning to Epping, Mister Boisjoly?" countered Livesy.

"Yes, good point, well made," I conceded. "Perhaps we could come to some sort of arrangement."

"All I want to know..." Livesy fixed his gaze onto Vickers' glassy eyes "...is how Mister Vickers says I got locked into the feed shed. I'll give you ten-to-one it don't line up with what you said."

"I'll take five pounds of that," bid Uncle Pim. "You'll carry me won't you, Anty?"

"Well, Mister Vickers?" prompted Livesy.

Vickers peered at the oatmeal purist over his stacks of packs. He glanced at me and then around the room. His eyes told the story of a man who not only didn't know the answer but had already forgotten the question.

"Yes, Mister Livesy?"

"How is it you suppose I came to be locked in my feed shed?"

Vickers stared at him blankly. Then he looked at me and his eyes told a different tale. This was no longer just a man who didn't know the answer to the question — although he was most certainly that — but he was also a man who knew Anty Boisjoly as well as anyone possibly could. The baffled panic fell away from his countenance like a pumpkin off a balcony, leaving only the aloof British couth of the career Vickers.

"The horse, Mister Livesy," reported Vickers indulgently. "He's not to blame, of course. I expect he was startled by something. A bird, perhaps."

"Ha!" Uncle Pim clapped his hands together. "The season's off to a good start."

"If you please, Mister Livesy." Vickers manoeuvred to the table and laid out the bounty.

In moments, a Christmas-morning warming supervened, as jolly old Saint Vickers passed out Iberian ham, scones and clotted cream, *terrine de porc,* and lashings and lashings of etc.

"Would you care to have your moment now, Mister Boisjoly?" Ivor, it should be noted, was uncharacteristically dripping wet from the hastily prepared search in heavy weather, and even more uncharacteristically cheery about it all, as he slowly and luxuriously tamped down a pipe overflowing with Dunhill. He had removed my swallowtail coat and hung it carefully on the floor to dry.

"Surely it's all obvious now, Inspector — ah, thank you Vickers." I welcomed a brass travel tumbler of warm whisky and rainwater. "Doctor Smick and Colonel Brimble were killed by their vices."

"Doctor Smick had no vices," protested Nurse Dalimore.

"I'm afraid he did," I gently corrected, "and the one person who knew about it was Sir Melvin, who accidentally mentioned seeing the doctor at a dining and smoking club called Belle Arome which, as Colonel Brimble later told us, has a strict non-non-smoking policy. Sir Melvin saw Smick there smoking and, in all likelihood, drinking."

"The very height of…" Sir Melvin popped the lid off a tin of caviar, "…hypocrisy. But I didn't kill him — if he weren't a smoker he'd be fine now. I mean to say, not fine — he'd still be a diabolical despot, but he'd be alive."

"The spent cigarettes that we found in the compound after the murder weren't smoked by a killer up a tree with a poison dart, they were poisoned cigarettes smoked by Doctor Smick and then discarded into the wind which, you'll recall, Inspector, would always be blowing against anyone trying to aim a poison dart. That same wind carried the murder weapon away from the scene of the crime," I explained, "where Sir Melvin had placed them at Doctor Smick's disposal."

"But, why?" Nurse Dalimore lamented. "Why even bring poisonous cigarettes to Eden Bliss Paradise?"

"To give Smick the same choice he offered me — to either live by his ideologies or die by his vices," mumbled Sir Melvin through a mouthful of caviar and toast. "I came here to get well, and instead I got thin. Then he sent me back to get fat again. Then thinner again. Then fatter. Every time I was more ravenous than the last." Sir Melvin swallowed and then stared wide-eyed into an astonishing past. "I chartered a ship. A whole ship, just for one meal. The man was breaking me."

Ivor stoked his pipe up to a steam engine ideal before asking the obvious, "Why not just stop coming to Eden Bliss Paradise?"

"That was the fiendish hold he had over all of us." Sir Melvin took in his fellow inmates with a fevered glare. "He hooked us on health, but only so long as we paid for it. And then, when I saw him there at the Belle Arome, smoking cigarettes and drinking whisky…"

"And what had Colonel Brimble to do with any of it?" Ivor watched a new leak open directly above my swallowtail coat.

"That was an accident," contended Sir Melvin as he contended with a tin of potted salmon.

"The poisonous whisky and cigarettes were hidden in the long sedge grass next to the pond," I explained. "I spotted them from the bee tree, which is the only place from which they could have been seen."

"And Colonel Brimble also climbed the tree, looking for honey," concluded Ivor.

"He did," I awarded the point with a tip of my tumbler. "He spotted the whisky and then, as soon as he felt he safely could, he rowed out to retrieve a bottle and was drinking it when we called to him. He affected not to notice us, at first, while he finished the bottle and then dropped it into the water."

"With what initiative?" scoffed Baroness Garlic. "The man never displayed an ounce more energy alive than he does dead. Probably less."

"The one thing that motivated Colonel Brimble to seek whisky was whisky," I explained. "I noticed that among the containers in his mead fermentorium was a flask, not unlike that which Diogenes made me empty before entering the compound. I expect the same thing happened to the colonel and, thusly inspired, he called upon his knowledge of mediaeval agriculture. When he spotted the honey tree, he fashioned a bee-becalming smoke-making device — which I later discovered in the tree and took for a blowpipe — and climbed up. He doubtless made several harvests and at some point he saw, as I did, the whisky that Sir Melvin had hidden in the sedge grass by the pond."

"So, in both cases, the victim disposed of the evidence," observed Babbage's cloud of smoke. "There was no poison dart?"

"No, no poison dart," I said to the disappointed cloud. "Not only would it have required marksmanship unparalleled in the history of poison darts, it wouldn't have been possible for anyone to have done it unseen."

Uncle Pim finished his teacup of straight whisky and handed it to Vickers for treatment. "How did you know that Sir Melvin was the culprit?"

"I'm not a culprit," claimed Sir Melvin. "I'm a provider. Not against the law, is it?"

"Of course it is," said Ivor.

"I'm not sure it is, Inspector," billowed Babbage.

"Only one person could have done it," I explained, nevertheless, "as indicated by the evidence of the hawthorn berry and the red dart."

"Noticed that, did you?" asked Sir Melvin.

"I did," I said. "Whoever smuggled cigarettes and whisky into Eden Bliss Paradise Health Resort must have known that Diogenes had no sense of smell."

"The dog can't smell?" gabbled just about everyone as a unit. Diogenes, who sat next to Henny, carefully and systematically dismantling a Mowbray pork pie, cast an imperious eye over the room, as though to say, 'And what of it? At least I can see the plainly obvious.'

"He cannot, but only one person knew that — the man who was adding hawthorn berries to his porridge this morning," I said. "But the first and better clue was the missing red dart. The darts board, when I arrived, was provided with three blue darts and two red, a discrepancy which I initially took to be one of the many deviations of the games room. Later, however, Henny was pitting her three blue darts against Sir Melvin's three red. Later still, the board was reduced once again to two red darts. The drop and rise in the red dart population coincided on each occasion with the transportation of the bodies which, moments later, were found to have puncture marks."

"Not bees, then," presumed Pim.

"Not bees. Bees leave a stinger and, I can attest from recent personal experience," I held up my disfigured left hand, "a great red welt and a lingering sense of betrayal. No, these wounds were made, post-mortem, by throwing darts, and in the case of Colonel Brimble they were made amidships, the bit that was carried by Sir Melvin. His intention, obviously, was to distract us from the real manner in which the poison was delivered."

"I really just didn't want to go into the matter." Sir Melvin held aloft and gazed lovingly at a leg of roast pheasant. "I felt you had enough to contend with, what with all the death by misadventure and whatnot."

"I doubt very much that the coroner will find for death by misadventure," Ivor exhaled in a dubious plume.

"Might do," Babbage expelled in an ambiguous brume.

"At any rate, Sir Melvin, you must have known there'd be consequences," I said. "Why did you not endeavour to profit from the distraction as we searched for Miss Hackenit? You could have taken Clyde and a tremendous amount of quality nosh and been in Epping before we knew that you were gone."

"I could hardly let her drink poison just to prove she had the vices that Doctor Smick claimed he didn't." Sir Melvin regarded Henny over his pheasant leg. "She's the only honest one among us."

Diogenes wuffed a whispered accord with the sentiment and then accepted a scone from Henny's hand.

❦

"I'm going to call him Chipper." Henny referred, of course, to the former Diogenes, who sat admiring her from the floor of a first-class compartment rattling southwards from Epping. "Diogenes is far too dour a name for his new life on the estate."

Henny sat next to Vickers, who sat by the window in the direction of travel, as he always must do, or risk wakening with a start and the very concrete and surprisingly irretrievable impression that he's going backwards in time.

"Have you an estate, Henny?" I sat across from Henny and next to Uncle Pim, who sat across from Vickers, such that they both observed the sun glittering off the damp treetops of Epping Forest.

"I don't, but my maiden aunt's spread covers two hundred and fifty acres of East Sussex, with a lake, two gardens — one French and one English — a nine-hole golf course, a paddock, and a view of the Ouse from the south-east tower." Henny scratched the basset behind the ear. "But I believe Chip's going to be mainly an indoor dog. He's had enough of harsh elements, I feel."

"A most satisfactory conclusion, Miss, if I may take the liberty of expressing an opinion." Vickers nodded approval at Henny and Chip. "As is generally the case with Mister Boisjoly's adventures."

"Thank you, Vickers. I do my modest best and, as you know, refrain from singing my own praises." I waved a humble hand. "You, of course, are under no such restriction."

"Indeed, sir, I was about to comment that Baroness Garlic appeared most pleased with your observation that she required no legal apparatus to use the Smick method in light of the fact that there was no such thing."

"All bluff," I agreed. "And the copyright expired on bluff years ago."

"Similarly, Nurse Dalimore, I believe, found much pleasure in the arrangement she reached with the baroness to establish a larger, more luxurious, and better financed health resort," recounted Vickers. "She appeared to come into her own."

"The precise expression I'd have chosen, Vickers, if I were singing my own praises," I lauded. "She came neatly out from under the shadow of her infatuation with Doctor Smick."

"Even Mister Babbage appeared to take a renewed interest in his role as coroner," mused Vickers with somewhat less certainty, "particularly with respect to the delicate matter of whether or not Sir Melvin Otterwater is guilty of murder or some other offence."

"In any case, Mister Babbage and Inspector Wittersham enjoyed a smoke more than they've enjoyed anything else for years and years," I observed.

The forest gave way to suburb and the suburb soon to city, and Uncle Pim brooded on it all.

"Not such a satisfactory conclusion for me, though, Anty." He shook his head in a sort of fatigued disbelief. "Wait until your mother finds out that I was making book while at Eden Bliss."

"Need she find out?" I wondered.

"Don't you think it'll come out at the inquest?" Pim raised his eyebrows and his spirits, briefly, followed.

"Ah, yes. I suppose she will find out."

"She'll cut me off again," Pim predicted, accurately. "And make London uninhabitable."

"Can you not just give up gambling, Pim?" asked Henny. "I did. It was easy."

Pim looked at her sadly. "I cannot. My devotion to the demon odds runs too deep. I'm forever doomed to try to win back that which is lost forever." He once again gazed out the window at the intensifying city and visited new torments on his waistcoat button. "And to think it all started with a flip of a coin."

"What did?" asked Henny.

"Uncle Pim gambled away his chance with the woman he loved," I explained. "He risked and lost all on the toss of a coin."

"How very peculiar."

"Not very," I said. "Not by the standards of Uncle Pim, at any rate. He once bet a Gainsborough miniature on a nay outcome of a debate of the Oxford Union, to wit; 'This house holds that Cambridge should become a horticultural college.'"

"It only passed by a hundred and eighty votes," offered Pim in defence.

"But you didn't own a Gainsborough miniature, did you Unclington?" I reminded him, and then confided to Henny, "He had to purchase it at auction at considerable personal expense."

"That is peculiar," acknowledged Henny, "but that's not what I meant. I was referring to the peculiar coincidence that the same thing happened to my aunt."

"What did?" asked Pim. "Losing a sure thing on the Oxford Union debates or losing a Gainsborough she didn't have?"

"Losing the love of her life over the flip of a coin," said Henny. "Poor Aunty Sharmin. She failed to speak up and the man she loved wagered his chance with her on a coin toss. It broke her heart, and she never married."

"Aunty… Sharmin?" The penny began to drop for Uncle Pim. "Your aunt isn't Min Baffins."

"Why shouldn't she be?" asked Henny. "Someone has to be."

"But…" Pim paused while the engine tootled a warning to Liverpool Street Station to expect company. "Didn't she marry Taff Carmel?"

"The dimmest man in the Home Counties, not counting Berkshire," quoted Henny. "She used to call him Mooncalf Taff, when she was feeling generous. You're not telling me you're the oaf who lost your chance with her in a bet?"

"I am, indeed, the oaf in question."

"Astounding…" Henny appraised Pim as though in a new light. "I always assumed that your head would be much, much smaller, and that your eyes would never entirely work as a team."

"And she remained unmarried all these years…" marvelled Pim.

"As unmarried as the day you broke her heart for her," Henny assured him.

The steam brakes sighed and we twitched to a halt enveloped in vapour and fume. Presently, as it will, the fog dissolved from the platform to reveal, standing on her own, a sad-faced heiress with two hundred and fifty acres and a paddock. Pim rose slowly from his seat with sentiment glistening in his eyes and whispered, "Min."

Min Baffins blinked in disbelief and then stepped slowly, tentatively to the carriage window. She reached a delicately gloved hand to the glass.

"So long, Anty." Pim put on his hat and forgot his trunk and dashed from the carriage, and an instant later he was on the platform and folding in his arms the woman he'd lost all those years ago.

"Well, that explains the society pages." Henny nodded in agreement with the answer to some long-standing question. "Aunty Min wasn't saving stories about you — they were about your uncle, but somehow you were always mentioned."

"That happens rather a lot," I said. "It's also very common with regards to any reference to the Juniper Gentleman's Club, the Burlington Arcade, and whenever anyone — at all — skis down the escalator at Harrods."

"I'm sorry I missed those."

"Perhaps now you won't," I suggested. "If *my* Uncle Pim becomes *your* Uncle Pim, then not only will his anger issues be at an end, but you'll have all the society contacts you could possibly need. Why, you could come up before Bow Street Magistrates' twice a month, if you like. We could share a taxi."

"Do you think so, Anty?"

"It's just down to whether or not she'll take him back," I said. "Think she will?"

Henny regarded the scene on the platform and touched away a tear.

"I'll bet you anything."

Anty Boisjoly Mysteries

Thank you for reading *Death Reports to a Health Resort*. I hope you didn't work out too quickly who did it (assuming you tried) but even if you did you were able to do so with the clues to hand. Above all, I very much appreciate the investment of your time and reading budget, which I hope you felt was rewarded.

If you've read previous Anty Boisjoly Mysteries you may have noticed that this time the solution is deliberately (if only slightly) more straight-forward and cluey — only one person could have done it because of his proximity to the parts of the bodies that were punctured post-mortem — but that was easily missed, hence the narrative nudges in the form of, as only two examples, Erysichthon of Thessaly and the anecdote about the talking dog.

If you haven't read previous Anty Boisjoly Mysteries, please don't read the previous paragraph. Instead, have a look below at the... what is it, now? Eight? ...other books in the series, or skip to the end and sign up for the newsletter so you can be kept informed of pending new titles, exclusive insider information, cryptic clues, and cartoons.

The Case of the Canterfell Codicil
The frightful fate of the fourth earl of fray
In *The Case of the Canterfell Codicil,* Wodehousian gadabout and clubman Anty Boisjoly takes on his first case when his old Oxford chum and coxswain is facing the gallows, accused of the murder of his wealthy uncle. Not one but two locked-room mysteries later, Anty's matching wits and witticisms with a subversive butler, a senile footman, a single-minded detective-inspector, an irascible goat, and the eccentric conventions of the pastoral Sussex countryside to untangle a multi-layered mystery of secret bequests, ancient writs, love triangles, revenge, and a teasing twist in the final paragraph.

The Case of the Ghost of Christmas Morning
The affair of the phantom farewell
Anty Boisjoly visits Aunty Boisjoly, his reclusive aunt, at her cosy, sixteen-bedroom burrow in snowy Hertfordshire, for a quiet Christmas in dairy country. But even before he arrives, a local war hero has not only been murdered in a most improbable fashion, but hours later he's standing his old friends Christmas drinks at the local.

The only clues are footprints in the snow, leading to the only possible culprit — Aunty Boisjoly.

The Tale of the Tenpenny Tontine
The dual duel dilemma
It's another mystifying, manor house murder for bon-vivant and problem-solver Anty Boisjoly, when his clubmate asks him to determine who died first after a duel is fought in a locked room. The untold riches of the Tenpenny Tontine are in the balance, but the stakes only get higher when Anty determines that, duel or not, this was a case of murder.

The Case of the Carnaby Castle Curse
Bones, stones, and crones;
what moans alone in the catacombs
The ancient curse of Carnaby Castle has begun taking victims again — either that, or someone's very cleverly done away with the new young bride of the philandering family patriarch, and the chief suspect is none other than Carnaby, London's finest club steward.

Anty Boisjoly's wits and witticisms are tested to their frozen limit as he sifts the superstitions, suspicions, and age-old schisms of the mediaeval Peak District village of Hoy to sort out how it was done before the curse can claim Carnaby himself.

Reckoning at the Riviera Royale

The relevance of the evidence of the reticence of elephants

Anty finally has that awkward 'did you murder my father' conversation with his mother while finding himself in the ticklish position of defending her and an innocent elephant against charges of impossible murder.

If that's not enough, Anty's fallen for the daughter of the mysterious mother-daughter team of gamblers, there's a second impossible murder, and Anty has a very worrying idea who it is that's been cheating the casino.

The Case of the Case of Kilcladdich

Will a still still still still?

Anty Boisjoly travels to the sacred source waters of Glen Glennegie to help decide the fate of his favourite whisky, but an impossible locked room murder is only one of a multitude of mysteries that try Anty's wits and witticisms to their northern limit.

Time trickles down on the traditional tipple as Anty unravels family feuds, ruptured romance, shepherdless sheep, and a series of suspiciously surfacing secrets to sort out who killed whom and how and why and who might be next to die.

Foreboding Foretelling at Ficklehouse Felling

The medium with the message of the most perilous of presage

It's Anty's reddest-of-herringed, twistiest-of-turned, locked-roomiest manor house mystery yet, when a death is foretold by a mystic that Anty's sure is a charlatan. But when an impossible murder follows the foretelling, Anty and his old ally and nemesis Inspector Wittersham must sift the connivance, contrivance, misguidance, and reliance on pseudoscience of the mad manor and its oddball inhabitants before the killer strikes again.

Mystery and Malice Aboard RMS Ballast

Tales of sails and betrayals and for some reason mails

Anty, Vickers, Inspector Wittersham, and a passenger list of howling eccentrics find themselves prey to the sway and spray of the Scilly Seas when what at first seems a simple, unexplainable, locked-state-room murder twists into a tale of buried treasure, perilous weather and dangerous endeavours at sea.

Death Reports to a Health Resort

The case of the case of withdrawal

We meet more of Anty's eccentric extended family when he visits his uncle at a retreat for fans of the first deadly sin and enthusiasts of the sixth. Motivated suspects are plump and plentiful when the most disliked man in the spa is the victim of a locked room murder, but Inspector Wittersham soon points the finger at Anty's uncle and things only get worse when a second murder occurs that both eye-witnesses — Anty Boisjoly and Ivor Wittersham — swear was impossible.

Teddy Quillfeather Mysteries

Anty's fast-thinking, faster-talking, and even faster-acting cousin Teddy Quillfeather was first sighted in *Mystery and Malice aboard RMS Ballast* and almost immediately she decided she'd like to have her own series.

She's not mad for murder, though, is our Teddy, and indeed her hands-on, all-in, everything-down style of problem-solving is best suited to the manor-house heist, race-track diddle, and high-stakes fiddle, and Teddy's as likely to be the author of the multitude of country-house capers as are the culprits.

Hardy Haul at Hardy Hall

The first ever Teddy Quillfeather!
The theft of an immensely valuable, immensely ugly necklace is only the beginning of the intrigues and oddities at a country weekend at Hardy Hall where Teddy Quillfeather's mother has sent her with strict instructions to select an eligible bachelor from a shortlist of aristocrats, eccentrics, and egos.

But when Teddy sets out to discourage the suitors and discover the looters with her natural knack for applied shenanigans she instead uncovers countless conspiracies, complicated by country house courtesies. It's a comedy of manners and caper of manors and the only solution, if you're Teddy Quillfeather, is obviously another heist.

Frauds On Favourite

Teddy's at the track and the odds are odder than ever.

Teddy's off to the races in this multi-layered multiplier mystery of dark horses and dodgy courses, pawky jockeys, unstable stables, impossible odds, crooked bookies, and a track-wide conspiracy to deny the punter an even chance. That's more than enough to invite a counter-con from Teddy, but when the family paddock is implicated in race-fixing, she does what she does best when the odds go against her — she raises the stakes.

Beyond the backmatter

Anty minds the locked room murders while Teddy handles heists and vice and counterfeit ice, and to help keep track of it all, plus cryptic clues and custom content and cartoons confined to the club, you can sign up for the combined Boisjoly/Quillfeather Infrequent Newsletter…

http://indefensiblepublishing.com/newsletters/

Made in the USA
Las Vegas, NV
28 September 2024

95927775R00132